Iva-Marie Palmer

GABBY GARCIA'S
ULTIMATE PLAYBOOK

MVP SUMMER

Illustrations by Marta Kissi

D0108266

KATHERINE TEGEN BOOKS
An Imprint of HarperCollins Publishers

Katherine Tegen Books is an imprint of HarperCollins Publishers.

Gabby Garcia's Ultimate Playbook #2: MVP Summer
Copyright © 2018 by HarperCollins Publishers
Emoji icons provided by EmojiOne
All rights reserved. Printed in the United States of America.
No part of this book may be used or reproduced in any manner
whatsoever without written permission except in the case of brief
quotations embodied in critical articles and reviews. For information
address HarperCollins Children's Books, a division of HarperCollins
Publishers, 195 Broadway, New York, NY 10007.
www.harpercollinschildrens.com

ISBN 978-0-06-239183-4

Typography by Katie Fitch
18 19 20 21 22 CG/LSCH 10 9 8 7 6 5 4 3 2 1
❖
First Edition

GABBY GARCIA'S

ULTIMATE PLAYBOOK

MVP SUMMER

To my father, Bill Palmer, who took me to my first baseball game, and who taught me that when you're playing, you're already winning. You're one of my life's MVPs if there ever was one.

GABBY GARCIA'S
ULTIMATE PLAYBOOK

MVP SUMMER

Whew. I just want to tell you, playbook, that I didn't forget about you. That's why I started with "whew." It's been busy.

Is it weird to talk to you like a person I'm catching up with? (That's what Louie says when she has a friend drop by for a visit: "I need to catch up with you!" But they're not racing. Usually drinking wine. Sometimes they also have a strange platter of veiny and stinky cheeses and dried fruits that look like oversized boogers if you ask me. Gross. I vow to stick with Capri Sun and Doritos for life. Anyway . . .)

But. Okay. Well.

I'll call it a recap. It's not a replay 'cause I can't get into **EVERY** detail. Like I said, I was busy. And now I'm tired. And still busy! (I'm getting to that!)

But I had that whole thing happen where the Penguins won our playoff game to head to regionals. On that same day, we also found out that the Piper Bell Talent Squad had earned enough online votes to go to New York City for a national talent show.

AND THEN my crush Johnny Madden, who made it pretty obvious he likes me back (I **THINK**?), told me Luther was going to reopen

for the end of the school year and it seemed like I would have to go back and miss participating with either Piper Bell team.

It was a lot to process, believe me. Of course, playbook, you think that's because of the crush thing, but I am not stereotypical that way. The crush had to wait: I had a conundrum. A three-pronged conundrum.

I won't even try to find the right words to describe the feeling I had. It was a feeling of really not wanting a conundrum. (Does anyone?) Because I'd spent two months trying to make Piper Bell work for me and when it finally was, Luther had to go and mess with my head.

But all that recapping is mainly important for dramatic effect because, well, first, some very intelligent adult said that even if Luther could reopen (asbestos-free!), it wouldn't be good for so many students who'd already "endured a period of adjustment" by switching to different schools just two months before to have to switch back for the last two weeks of the school year. They should really give adults prizes for that kind of reasonable thinking.

Conundrum Prong A fell away.

But I still had the regional game and New York to choose between. They were happening on the same day. In other words, two things at once. Which, let's face it, playbook, wasn't an ideal situation, as there is only one of me.

So then I had a decision. And, as many of the earlier pages I wrote can show, I wasn't exactly great at those. Or maybe I chose things for the wrong reasons (play field hockey for fame and glory, anyone?). But this time, I decided in less than a minute.

IT. WAS. SO. WEIRD. It was the world record, I bet, for making a tough decision.

Because, first, for maybe twenty seconds, I imagined New York and TV and reading my awesome heartfelt poem on TV in front of a live studio audience, and people calling in to vote for me and maybe even some viewers at home deciding they might want to be poets, too, just like Gabby Garcia. (Hey, it happens all the time when people watch a baseball game; why not poetry?)

But then, it dawned on me. Poetry, even though I loved it, was only my new thing because I'd been denying my true love for, well, my true love: **BASEBALL**. So I knew I had to go play in that game.

And, well . . .

THE REASON FOR MY ABSENCE: THE ATLANTA-AREA MIDDLE SCHOOL REGIONALS

A Replay

Okay, the real reason I kind of dropped off writing for a while is that . . . well . . .

Fine, so we lost. The Penguins lost.

Deep down, I didn't really think we'd lose. And after spending my entire time at Piper Bell trying to figure out my place in everything, I thought somehow that the universe would tell me that all my decisions had been the right ones and we would win. (That would be the universe talking to me.)

Ugh, and that wasn't what all my learning was about!

4

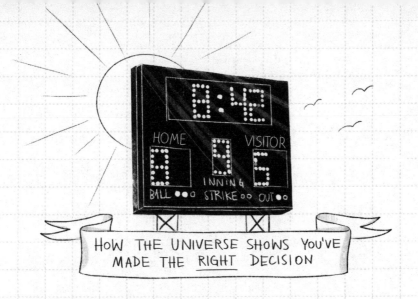

HOW THE UNIVERSE SHOWS YOU'VE
MADE THE RIGHT DECISION

Because I **DID** figure out there are more important things than winning and I **DO** believe that. I **DO**. But I'd be lying to write that it doesn't take some getting used to. When you lose, you might gain wisdom, but when you win, you get a **TROPHY**. Wisdom is nice and all but you just carry it around in your brain. Trophies get to go on a shelf and you can polish them and casually say, "Oh, that? Yes, that's my first place Atlanta-Area Middle School Regional Baseball Championship trophy. What a great game." There aren't as many casual opportunities to talk about the wisdom you gained.

And I gained a lot. Because, while we were losing, the talent squad (my field hockey teammates who are talented in a bunch of things that are not field hockey, which they're awful at) were kind of, sort of, winning. Well,

IMPRESSIVE TROPHY FOR TALENT NATIONALS!

becoming second runners-up. But in a national competition involving teams from every state, second runner-up is a big deal. Plus, they got trophies.

It's very hard to not think that being a big deal is a big deal. Especially when you end up trophy-less and know you could have wound up having one.

But this is a replay, so here goes. I was at the game. I wasn't pitching. Devon was the starting pitcher. I was fine with that, which is proof that I was doing good at not making everything all about me. And more proof is that, as I write this, I'm not going to blame Devon for the loss. The truth is, the opposing team was **GOOD**. Great, even. All my life I've been one of the best players in Peach Tree, Georgia, thinking I could compete on any playing field.

It turns out, there are even better players out there. Which, obviously, I know (I mean, look at Mo'ne Davis!). But I didn't know there were **SO MANY** good ones and so close to home. Like this team, from just outside Atlanta . . . as hard as it is to admit, they were better than us. And we were good enough to make it to regionals!

6

By the fourth inning, we were down 1–0, and by the sixth, 3–0. We weren't playing badly. Everyone was doing what they needed to do and Devon really was pitching great. It just so happened that the opponent, the Roosevelt Rhinos, were just hitting in bigger, better ways than Devon was pitching.

And **THEIR** pitcher, for the Rhinos? Well, he was great. He seemed to have pitches I never saw before, that don't even have names yet. **BUT**, and here's the crazy part: even though I usually pay most attention to opposing pitchers (it's hard not to when pitchers get to stand in the middle of the infield), it was the Rhinos' catcher who really wowed me.

She kept the innings moving fast, getting the ball right back to her pitcher. She threw signals for pitches that I totally agreed with (a lot of the time, I have to shake my catcher's signals off, and a lot of the time I'm right). She was everything I, as a pitcher, wanted in a catcher. (No offense to my past catchers, but it would have been great to be paired with her!)

At one point, Mario hit a ball straight up into the air, one of those hits that bashes the top of the backstop and zooms right down. She caught it like it was nothing, even though it hit her mitt so hard it had to hurt. Her team-mates surrounded her and said, "Awesome play!" and she just kind of smiled like she did that kind of thing every day.

THE AMAZING ROOSEVELT CATCHER + HER TEAMMATES

Maybe her whole life was like that: top-notch moments that she didn't even seem to think about. I wondered if she kept a playbook what it would be like. And then I thought maybe some people didn't even need playbooks. I think I am not one of those people: even if you can glide through life, it can't hurt to think where you want to glide **TO**, right?

In the seventh inning, Coach Hollylighter put me in as Devon's reliever. I had a moment out there where maybe things could have turned around—I'd let someone on base and then the next batter came up and hit a little waffly unsure hit.

The ball came right to me and I scooped it up and tossed it to Davey Herring at second, who should have tagged up his base and quickly thrown it to Mario at first. Easy double play, two outs. And, the kind of thing that can totally change the mood and the way a game is going. Instead, Davey grabbed the ball and looked around, like he'd forgotten the right moves. By the time he tagged out the runner to second base, the batter was already on first.

It happens. It happens, it happens, it happens, I had to keep telling myself. And I'm **STILL** telling myself. As much as I wanted to tell Davey what the right move would have been, I didn't. Because I think he already knew so I let it go. Why would I want to make Davey feel worse, right?

Still, even after the bad play, I got this really excellent feeling that we could win—I don't know why, just sometimes this idea gets in my head and I can almost **SEE** points on the scoreboard that aren't there yet. So in the dugout, I got everyone around me and said: "Okay, they might have the lead. They might have some tricks up their sleeves that we don't know about. They wouldn't be here if they didn't. But neither would we. What we have is, we're **US**. The Piper Bell Penguins. Penguins! Who would name a baseball team after a cold-weather bird that doesn't fly? **BUT**, the secret of all victory is in the non-obvious."

That last part was a Marcus Aurelius quote that my dad says to himself when he's pacing around, trying to find an angle for a story he's writing. He would have liked my speech. The team seemed to, or at least that part about the penguins got a laugh.

But . . .

Even though great speeches involving penguins and dead-people quotes **SHOULD** make all the difference in the world, well . . .

We never quite had a comeback, even though I believed we would. Sigh. This replay is not very fun to replay.

The Rhinos catcher was the MVP for the game. (They ended up winning 4–0.) She got a one-run homer in the ninth, and she didn't even make a huge deal about it. She was **HAPPY**, for sure, but she almost seemed like she had somewhere even better to go right after the game. (And where could be better than a place where you're wearing an MVP medal and helping hold your team's fresh, shiny trophy?!)

She probably had some amazing summer plans to get to. Maybe skydiving without looking terrified. Or like petting sharks as if they were puppies. Meanwhile, I had no summer plans. Or nothing spectacular planned, anyway. Diego and I had planned to have an MVP Summer before eighth grade started, but he's still in Costa Rica.

I'm trying to fight off the feeling that this loss (especially after thinking it could be a **WIN**) is the start of a streak, even though I know since I started this playbook, I can't think about things that way.

I found out that win streaks don't mean anything if you can't hold on to them, and it's almost better to accept that you'll win some games and lose some. In fact, someone once said, "you win some, you lose some." Weirdly, I can't find out who, even though it's a pretty good thing to have said.

I bet whoever it was kept a highly detailed life playbook, huh?

GOOD THINGS PEOPLE SAID
BUT NO ONE IS SURE WHO

- To be a winner, all you need to give is all you have.

- Today is the tomorrow you worried about yesterday.

- Where there's a will, there's a way.

- Two wrongs don't make a right.

WHAT ELSE I'VE BEEN DOING: A HIGHLIGHT REEL

(The following is color commentated by Bob and Judy, the sportscasters who live in my head (and are really just figments of my imagination)—**NOSY SPY READING THIS—(THAT MEANS YOU, PETER!!)—DON'T MAKE THIS A BIG DEAL!)**

Bob: Well, Gabby and the Penguins may have lost the regional game, but that didn't leave her short of any scorching early summer action.

Judy: I know, Bob; the next day, after the Penguin talent squad returned from New York, Gabby had to quickly prep an outfit for a celebratory barbecue!

Bob: Not just an outfit; she brought dip! Her dad's famous

TRADITIONAL BBQ LOOK

FANCY GARDEN BBQ LOOK

Guacamole Castle. Let's just say the talent squad treated it so royally that castle didn't last long.

Judy: She really scored big on that.

Bob: And Piper Bell graduation was bittersweet for her. She's set to return to her home team of Luther next year. What will that mean for all the alliances she's formed at Piper Bell?

Judy: Let's not get too far ahead of ourselves, Bob. She'll have the summer to readjust . . .

Bob: To what she used to be adjusted to?

Judy: Bob, you're getting too think-y. Let's cut to another highlight: Gabby

WE HAVE A WINNER BBQ LOOK

got asked out on her first official date!

Bob: That was awkward but also quite a play on Johnny Madden's part!

Judy: Don't give him all the credit: things could have gone either way when he smashed into Gabby with that plate full of dip.

Bob: I thought that was intentional.

Judy: Well, what's key here is that Gabby said yes!

Bob: I really hope we can catch the replay.

THE REASON FOR THE SEASON IS AWESOMENESS (I HOPE?)

Summer
A Preseason Game Plan*
June 18
*Preseason game plans are BIGGER than plays, BTW.

I've been lounging around for two days now. It's something people do, but I don't really do it. It's a strange feeling, to be reclined on the couch, watching baseball but not really watching. It could be golf for all the attention I'm paying. (No, if it were golf, I'd be asleep.)

My dad is editing a book for someone, so he's on deadline. Louie just had to drop Peter off someplace. My cat, Koufax, keeps sauntering in and out of the room and looking at me, like he doesn't really want to hang out with me.

I feel a little . . . strange. Not sick or anything but off somehow. My date with Johnny is tomorrow, and I'm a little nervous about it—but also excited: like who knew that with a boy you like, if your hands touch for a second because you're helping him to clean guacamole off his shirt, it's like you hit three grand slams and pitched a no-hitter all while being spun around in one of those cotton-candy machines until you're just a flossy, floating pastel smile version of yourself?! But the date is not why I'm off. It's more that I just don't know what to do with myself.

I think it's because of the MVP Summer and how it's not going to happen now. Oh yeah, the MVP Summer: a few weeks ago, when I **THOUGHT** my best friend, Diego Parker, would be getting back from Costa Rica, I was looking through a box of old baseball stuff and found a ticket stub from a Braves game we went to when we were ten. I remembered it perfectly: me and Diego had been kicked back in our seats talking about when we'd be older and we decided that the summer before we turned thirteen would be our best ever. (I don't know if he remembered, but then I'd thought how I'd plan it out and **SURPRISE** him and call it an **MVP SUMMER**.) Ugh. Then I found out that same day he's not going to be back for a while. He was **SUP-POSED** to come back until his dad got asked to stay and teach a course for a scientist who is leaving for a new study.

But this had been the plan: We had seen a group of teenagers and wondered if we'd still hang out as much when we got to be their age. Then Diego said how it was possible life would get way busier after eighth grade, so we should pack the summer before with memories and moments to cement our friendship for **ALL TIME**. And the capper to the summer Diego and I had discussed long ago was our joint thirteenth birthday party featuring all of our favorite things. I still have the **ORIGINAL LIST OF ACTIVITIES** we made (they were on the back of a scorecard. The Braves beat the Pirates 9–3 that day).

(**OLD ME**, if you're reading this and have forgotten some things, Diego and I were born a day apart in the hospital and his mom and my mom became good friends almost instantly. And when my mom died, Diego's family really helped out.)

That's the thing. Diego and I aren't any old best friends, or best friends who met in kindergarten or something. We are best friends *from birth*. (He's a day older, but who's counting?) When I think about our years of friendship, there are a million memories.

But if he's not here: No memories. No moments. No cake-based celebration. At least not the ones we'd planned on. This is like a rain-delayed ball game, quadrupled. No! It's like a whole baseball season being rained out.

Oh, I think I hear Louie.

(entry resumed after Louie talk)

So, I wasn't crazy, thinking I was off. Louie just came through the living room and, like Koufax, she, too, paused and looked at me for a minute. Unlike him, she asked to sit down by me, and I sat up on the couch to make room. "You okay?" she said.

My normal response to this is to always say that of course I'm okay, but today for some reason, I said, "What do you mean?" As if "you okay?" is a hard question.

"You just seem a little . . . untethered . . . for you." After peering at me with Concerned Mom Face for a moment, she added, "I know you've been busy since school let out, so it's okay to rest, but you can talk to me about whatever you need to."

CONCERNED MOM FACE:

1. LINE BETWEEN EYEBROWS

2. TILTED HEAD

3. HAND ON CHIN

"Okay," I said. I was not making this easy for her.

She patted my knee and pointed out that the Braves were at bat, then said, "Just keep me posted."

Can I be serious for a minute?

Under normal circumstances, this might not feel like the worst thing ever. I mean, I'll play baseball. I'll do summer-y things. I have new friends and the cotton-candy feeling with Johnny (that I hope he also has!). But after the last few months at Piper Bell, when I had a goal of getting my win streak back, I had a purpose. I may have gone about it a little wrong, but I ended up somewhere good.

And right now, I **AM** "untethered," or really, more like a free agent, which is a player who doesn't have a contract and can choose what team he or she wants to go to. That sounds exciting, but sometimes free agents don't wind up anywhere.

Now that the big parties and end-of-school commotion has passed, a lot of my Piper Bell friends left for family trips and things, at least for the beginning of summer. Johnny's around but that's different because, all the awesome-sweet feelings aside, well, I'm trying to figure out how it's different to "like like" a boy and not just like a boy (the way I like Diego). Katy Harris, one of my closest Piper Bell friends, is an even bigger celebrity now after the talent

19

showcase on TV, so she's also pretty busy.

Plus, okay, I'm a little sad, to be honest, that I won't be going back to Piper Bell in the fall. Now that Luther is reopened, I'll go there. Piper Bell Academy is expensive. There's a small chance that they might offer me a scholarship, but they told Dad and Louie that it would only happen if someone who was offered a scholarship turned it down. And, besides, even if I found a way to go there, Luther is where I belong. Right?

I think my pen sighed while I was writing this. Ugh. I don't mean to be so dramatic! But what else are you supposed to be when you're lolling around on the couch, wondering about your teenage future?

What if my Piper Bell friends are so busy this summer, they forget all about me when I go back to Luther? What if Johnny's fingers lightly touch mine and all **HE** feels is, like, a weird burping sensation? What if Diego stays in Costa Rica forever?

When it seemed like he was coming back, my summer was on solid ground. But now, that untethered idea sort of weirds me out: like, what if I float away?

At least baseball starts soon—I'm on the first-ever Peach Tree All-Star team and I am pumped about that.

But I need more than games to play. Here's the thing: this is a playbook. I need a play. A game plan.

Sometimes in a baseball game, a batter hits a high pop fly and everyone figures the pitcher will catch it. But when the sun is bright, sometimes you lose sight of the ball—you can't see it and you miss it or drop it.

Hmm. Right now, my whole life is that ball in the sun. I can't quite see it and I definitely don't want to miss it.

I need a mission, or a goal, but I don't know what it should be. I only know that I want to keep up with my playbook, and be true to myself, blah blah blah. One thing I know for sure is, the Best Me isn't this couch me. So, I definitely need to **DO SOMETHING**. A **FUN** something. But what? I'm sure a wise person would say, be your own best friend, but me and Diego would agree that sounds totally lame.

Koufax is back, looking at me again. He probably has all the answers, but of course I don't speak Cat.

THE GREATS: SANDY KOUFAX

Baseball Hall of Fame Pitcher for the Brooklyn/Los Angeles Dodgers (1955–1966), Number 32

From: Brooklyn, New York

Born: December 30, 1935

Best Season: 1963! He led the league in wins with 25, in shutouts with 11, and in strikeouts with 306. He won both the Cy Young Award and Most Valuable Player Award that season. (Though in 1965, he threw a record 382 strikeouts in one season!!)

What Yogi Berra Said: "I can see how he won twenty-five games. What I don't understand is how he lost five."

Fun Fact: When he was first coming up the major league ranks, he struggled to control his pitches and teammates joked he could barely keep his throws inside the batting cages. Some people even say that he would have been dropped if he was playing today, since most of his best games were in the second part of his career! He said, "I became a good pitcher when I stopped trying to make them miss the ball and started trying to make them hit it."

BIG SCREEN SCENE

First Date Goal: To not spook myself from ever wanting to go on a date again.

First Date Strategy: Not think of the date as a date. (Is that possible with all these **FEELINGS**?)

Post-Day Analysis: June 19

I'd never been on a real date before. I mean, I'm twelve going on thirteen, so that alone is not unusual. But leave it to my up-on-all-trends dad to throw me for a loop as I was getting ready to go with Johnny Madden to the newest Pizzabird movie. Before my dad mentioned "trends," I was focusing my worries on whether *Pizzabird* would end up being what its trailers promised it would be: the inspiring and amazing story of a pigeon that gets in touch with its ancient pigeon soul and becomes a carrier of pizza to a world in need. (It was, but I'm getting to that.)

Anyway, I'd felt better this morning than I had yesterday, mainly because I had somewhere to be. As I was getting ready, which to me meant asking my dad to put my hair in a braid instead of its usual ponytail, my dad asked me, "So this isn't a big group date? I read that's how your generation does things?" (Beware any grown-up questions that contain the words "your generation.")

"Huh?"

MINUS ONE FIRST-DATE POINT FOR GABBY FOR TOTAL CONFUSION AND WEIRD SEASICK FEELING!

"I've read several trend pieces on how one-on-one dating is a lost art for teenagers," he said. I was somewhat uncomfortable that he used the word *dating* and even the word *teenager* but also I really wanted to know what he meant. "Kids today go out in groups, or just sit and text each other while they hang out at someone's house. Everything is very casual."

"Hmm," was all I could think to say. I tried to check my dad's expression in the mirror as he worked on my braid, but I couldn't get a sense of what he was thinking. He seemed very normal and my-dad-like. "I guess Johnny didn't read that article."

DAD'S HAIR STYLES

HE CALLS THIS HIS CALLING. I AGREE ☺

"BRAID"

I HAVE NOW ✦ MASTERED ✦

RESERVED FOR WHEN I'M ELDERLY OR A LIBRARIAN

"BUN"

NOW LOUIE'S JOB BECAUSE SHE HAS HAIR TOOLS

"PONYTAIL"

RETIRED AT AGE 9

"HOLIDAY" (OR SPECIAL OCCASION HAIR)

"PIGTAILS"

"Well, good for him." Most kids my age might feel weird about discussing a date with their dads but I've always talked to mine about everything. There'd been a hiccup when I first started at Piper Bell and I hadn't wanted to tell him that the leftovers he was packing in my lunch were making me feel out of place, but now things were smooth sailing again.

Thankfully, after my hair was done, Dad dropped the dating talk and we listened to sports radio on the way to the movie theater—it kind of calmed my nerves. Until I saw Johnny waiting with the tickets just outside the movie theater. Sure, I'd *intended* to think of the date as a not-date for maximum comfortability, but Johnny totally screwed that up. Because he looked **REALLY CUTE**.

We hadn't talked much since the party when he'd asked me out in the first place, so you'd think we'd have a lot to say to one another immediately, but all the cotton-candy feelings made my mouth and brain like real

REALLY CUTE JOHNNY

cotton candy: sticky and sugary and spinny. I worried if I tried to say something, a million random things would come out.

MINUS ONE POINT FOR GABBY FOR WORD-MUSH MOUTH!

PLUS ONE POINT FOR JOHNNY FOR CAUSING WORD-MUSH MOUTH!

"So, Pizzabird?" Johnny said, looking somewhere over my shoulder. His cheeks were bright pink. Cotton-candy pink. Did that mean he knew the feeling?

PLUS ONE POINT FOR GABBY MAKING JOHNNY FEEL THE COTTON-Y FEELING

MINUS ONE POINT FOR JOHNNY BEING SO COTTON-Y HE COULDN'T THINK OF THINGS TO SAY, EITHER!

It took me a second to figure out that *Pizzabird* was not a strange code word and to remember it was the name of the movie we were seeing.

"Yeah, okay, Pizzabird!" I said. My voice sounded normal enough but my whole body was sort of vibrating. I wondered if I looked blurry to Johnny.

"This Pizzabird is supposed to be the best one yet," Johnny said as he held the first door open to me.

I held the next door open for him. "Yeah, I've seen the first Pizzabird movie five times."

We were saying *Pizzabird* so much. There was probably a limit on how many times you could say *Pizzabird* in a five-minute span. But the good thing was, we were saying **SOMETHING** and not letting the cotton-candy sensation stop our date progress.

"We shouldn't bother with snacks, right?" Johnny said as we walked in.

WHAT??? My not-filled-with-snacks stomach plummeted. Of course we should bother with snacks! Snacks weren't a bother! They were very important! What did this mean? If I told Johnny that going snackless sounded like a horrible idea, was the date over? I didn't want it to be over!

He laughed. "You look terrified. I was totally kidding," he said. "I wouldn't know why you agreed to this if I was anti-snack."

Because your eyes are very green and your smile is nice and that was a pretty funny trick to play, I thought but didn't say. Little emoji hearts might have been shooting from my eyes, though.

"That was really mean! I love movie snacks!" I said instead. And Johnny smiled again and so did I and we sort of stood there smiling at each other until an older man behind us said, "If you two don't hurry up, my coupon for a free Icee is going to expire."

ONE POINT EACH TO GABBY AND JOHNNY FOR BEING SO DISTRACTED BY SMILES THAT WE DIDN'T NOTICE AN OLD PERSON! (That's good, in this case.)

We agreed to order the biggest popcorn and Twizzlers after the near no-snacks scare. "Extra butter, please," Johnny and I said at the same time and I liked that he said please and also that we both wanted extra butter, even if there's no way that stuff is butter. There was definite **PERFECT MATCH** potential in the air. And the potential smelled like popcorn!

But then the perfect popcorn gave way to the worst thing ever: my brother, Peter, walked in. Well, Peter and his friends walked in. He'd gone to Jared's for the day and Jared's mom must have been ready to sit down in the dark so they couldn't see how exasperated she looked, because there they were: a pester of eight-year-olds. (Like a herd of cattle or a flock of sheep.)

MINUS ONE POINT FOR A LITTLE-BROTHER INTRU-SION!

"We should get seats!" I exclaimed to Johnny like it might be an emergency. It was, even if he didn't know it yet. I almost grabbed his hand to run and pull him to safety but then I realized I would have been holding his hand. Hand-holding required more of a lead-up, right?

"Yeah, let's go!" Johnny, I noticed, was talking much more loudly than usual.

I think we both had a case of first-date yips. Unlike normal yips, you don't feel like you've forgotten how to be you but instead your usual you-ness is sort of trapped under a Date Layer that's blushy and sweaty and shy and excited all at the same time. But the layer makes it harder to know if you're getting through to your date.

I pointed to some seats near the front—"Those look great," Johnny said in such a nice way that my internal scoreboard awarded me a point even if I hadn't really done anything—but not too near and we settled into them and for one second, Johnny's arm touched my arm on the armrest and I became dizzy **COTTON CANDY**. We both sprung apart and sort of laughed nervously, like we were about to go on a terrifying amusement park ride.

I peeked backward, thinking I was home free and Peter, et cetera, hadn't noticed me. Or better, had gone to another movie. But then I heard his voice, which made sweat leap out of my forehead and turned my fizzy happiness into a rocky puke sensation. (Just as awful as it sounds.) "I can't believe Robofang was sold out," Peter was saying. "Pizzabird better not stink. I could be doing something way better with my time."

UGH.

"That kid is pretty annoying," Johnny whispered. **WE HAD SO MUCH IN COMMON!**

ONE POINT EACH TO GABBY AND JOHNNY FOR MUTUAL ANNOYANCE WITH YOUNG MOVIEGOER.

BUT...

MINUS ONE POINT FOR GABBY WHEN HE FOUND OUT SHE WAS RELATED TO THE SOURCE OF ANNOYANCE?

Chomping on a Twizzler like it was my life's work, I said, or really, mumbled, "That kid is my brother."

Johnny looked like he'd just stepped on a kitten. "I'm sorry, I didn't know. I mean, he's not annoying. I've never been a big *Robofang* fan but I'm sure I'd be disappointed if I was and . . ."

I laughed and my heart thudded around because Johnny apologizing was as cute as Johnny smiling. "It's okay," I said. "I think he's annoying, too. You're 100 percent right."

"Oh good," Johnny said and his grin surpassed his

apology for its **VERY CUTENESS**. "The only thing worse than Robofang fans are disappointed Robofang fans."

And then things felt pretty easy for a few minutes as we munched popcorn and made funny faces at all the dumb things my brother and his friends were saying about Robofang's supremacy. Fun fact: if you are facing some first-date conversation jitters, communicating through facial expressions is a great solution!

Things were going **REALLY WELL**. But then, during the trailers, which everyone knows are one of the best parts of the movie experience, we were **SPOTTED**. "Isn't that your sister?" I heard Jared say.

"Ugh, yeah, and her **BOYFRIEND**, Johnny," Peter groaned loudly. I was sure Johnny heard because he got very still and seemed to be looking for the best kernel of popcorn to choose. Ugh, and it wasn't even like he was my **BOYFRIEND**. It was just one date.

I knew I'd gone into the first date without much of a strategy but Little-Brother Commentary was definitely **NOT** part of it. I wished that this *had* been a big group outing because with more people, there would be no way Peter and his pester could focus on how there were two of us, in a couple, sharing popcorn.

"Gabby and Johnny sitting on their butts, K-I-S-S-I-N-G, but I hope not because that's gross," Peter sang behind us, in a low whisper, not even bothering to get the words to a mocking poem right. AS a poet, it was doubly distressing.

And it wasn't like we were going to **KISS**. That I knew of. For that to happen, anyway, the date would have had to keep going well with talking or at least expressive face-talking, and the thing about your little brother and his friends mocking you from a few feet away is that you become self-conscious. Johnny and I had both frozen. Neither of us even reached for the popcorn. It was like an unspoken agreement to play dead so the predators would go away.

ONE POINT TO GABBY AND JOHNNY FOR AGREE-MENT ON A PLAY-DEAD STRATEGY!

MINUS ONE POINT FOR GABBY AND JOHNNY FOR NOT BREATHING PROPERLY!

But I managed to take one short breath through my teeth. I squeezed my hand in and out three times like I had my mitt on and was about to pitch. Okay. Having your little brother a few rows behind you at the movie was sort of like being on the mound or at bat when your opponent's fans started heckling you. If you paid too much attention to them, a terrible thing happened: you began to think about them and what they said—even dumb things like **"YOU SMELL!"** as if they could smell you from the stands.

Then you started to think it was true and then you began overthink and when that happened, you got the yips and the rest is very ugly history.

I already had first-date yips. Full-on yips would be unacceptable. They'd probably have to airlift a petrified me out of the theater.

"So, yep, that's my brother." I forced myself to say something. Peter wasn't going to heckle me and **WIN**.

"Isn't it better than if a random group of grade-school kids just followed you around to ruin your life?" Johnny said, coming to life again. Whew.

TWO POINTS TO GABBY AND JOHNNY FOR NOT DYING!

"You have a point. Sort of. Do you have siblings?" I asked Johnny, trying to ignore Peter and his merry band of cretins, who were making kissing noises. I wondered why Ms. Jared's Mom didn't tell them to calm down but a quick glance over my shoulder showed that she had her eyes closed,

TWO FACES OF GABBY

SMILEY FACE FOR JOHNNY

HORROR FACE FOR PETER

probably dreaming she was anywhere else in the world at that moment.

"An older sister," Johnny said. "She's in high school."

"Did you ever annoy her like this?"

"I don't think so," he said. "If I had, I think she would have killed me, and I'm still alive."

That was funny. And I laughed and then looked back at Peter with an evil face that said to cut it out.

"She's really cool. Her name is Sasha. She mostly makes it easy to be her little brother, but I think sometimes it's just that she doesn't even notice I'm there," he said. I found that hard to believe. Even if you had sisterly immunity to his **REALLY CUTE** smile, Johnny was super-brainy and nice and funny. Not someone to ignore.

"I let most things go with Peter," I said, half watching a trailer for the new Swift-Kick Sundae movie, about a group of ninjas who run an ice-cream truck and use it as a cover for their world-saving missions.

"Oh, so you're very Zen, then," Johnny said. "Did all that yoga Coach Raddock had the field hockey team do help you?"

"I'm not Zen at all," I said. "I just figure someday Peter will annoy someone so badly that they'll take care of him for me, so I let it go."

"That's also kind of Zen."

I didn't think of myself as very Zen, even if I was trying to do better. "How do some people get so calm? Like people who are beams of happy light and positivity. How?"

Johnny offered me some popcorn. He wasn't hogging it. I liked that. "Practice, probably, don't you think? Isn't everything people become good at just practice? Anyway, you're pretty positive."

Was he also saying I was like a beam of happy light? I sort of wanted that to be what he was trying to say. I also felt like I was riding a beam of light because we'd overcome the weirdness. It was almost easy, the date thing, except for every time Peter or one of his goons would mutter something from behind us. Like, "I'll vomit if they kiss." Or, "Do you think they're in love?"

Those things were somehow much worse than the K-I-S-S-I-N-G song, I think, because the song was like when opposing teams sang "Hey, batter batter, **SWING**!" but the chitchat felt more factual, or something. It made me sweaty (or sweatier) and each time I heard them, and knew Johnny had heard them, we both froze for several seconds and stared straight ahead at the screen like we had never met before and had just been dropped into the movie theater by aliens. It was not Zen at all. Unless being Zen involves a whole lot more secret sweating than I realized.

But then the movie started, and if anything can make a person stop worrying about the opinions of her eight-year-old brother and his friends, it's the story of Pizzabird. Pizzabird's main mission in life, after some initial good deeds, was trying to get a cranky old woman named Franny who used to run a pizza restaurant to start making pizzas again, because sharing her gift (and her pizza) with the world made everyone happy.

This was all fine and good, until Johnny held my hand.

HOW COULD I EVER BE ZEN WHEN HE WAS HOLD-ING MY HAND?

I was no longer cotton candy or pastel floss or a floating smile. I was laser beams going haywire. What did I do? Just hold his hand? Tell him I was sorry if my hand was sweaty? Did I get popcorn with my free hand? Did I use my free hand to high-five the universe because **JOHNNY MADDEN WAS HOLDING MY HAND**?

I had not prepared for this at all! One second, my hand was full of popcorn and the next second, Johnny was holding it. I Zen-ly tried to process it: His hands were cool and dry. He was looking straight ahead and the lights had dimmed, so I couldn't see if his cheeks were pink still. Maybe he'd grabbed my hand by accident?

I used my free hand to reach for some popcorn, careful not to disturb the other half of my body. But then Johnny let go of my hand and took a handful of popcorn.

I left my just-held hand on the armrest but nothing happened. I was very confused. Was it the butter? Or was hand-holding something you did on a clock, like when you had the ball in a basketball game and had to get rid of it before the buzzer sounded? I could barely focus on the movie's really exciting flight scene—Pizzabird being chased by a Health Department drone!—because I was trying to figure out what had gone wrong.

Bob: *I don't know if we'll see future matchups on the schedule, given how quickly Johnny ended that hand-holding play.*

Judy: *Bob, don't be silly. Gabby and Johnny clearly get along. No need to rush to conclusions. He could have just wanted more popcorn.*

Bob: *That might be a fair call.*

I very reasonably, very Zen-ly, told myself not to think about it too much. My cousin Jasmine who's in high school is what my parents called "boy-bonkers" and at family parties she never looks up from texting all her friends messages like, "What do you think he meant by 'hi'?"

It didn't seem fun to be like Jasmine. But it also wasn't fun wondering if my hand-holding skills needed work.

Who did you even ask about that kind of thing? On the screen, Pizzabird and Franny were feeding the neighborhood hot slices of pepperoni pie.

"That looks so good," I said. I didn't want to talk during the movie but all the wonders in my head were pushing words out of my mouth.

"Yeah, we should go for pizza sometime," Johnny whispered. He didn't hold my hand and say it, but at least he wanted to do something again.

POINT FOR POSSIBLE SECOND DATE! OR DID HE JUST MEAN HANG OUT SOMETIME?

When the lights came up, Peter muttered, "They're still here? Ugh," about me and Johnny (coincidentally, I was thinking the same thing about Peter and his friends). Johnny blushed as soon as I made eye contact with him. I got all fizzy inside and then I dropped what was left of my soda and ice went everywhere and when I crouched down to get it, so did he and our heads smashed together, **HARD**.

Did a shared head injury make a date good or bad? I wondered.

"I'm sorry!" I said, again too loudly, and I made a weird face I hoped Johnny would find funny and would understand immediately meant, **I REALLY LIKE YOU**. "This is why I don't really play contact sports." (That was a joke because I could handle most sports.)

"It's okay, I don't need my brain for summer vacation," Johnny said. Then he reached out and for a split second I was worried he was going to do something romantic with my hair—or maybe hoping he would—but also wishing I could make everyone else in the theater go away. He pulled a piece of popcorn out of my braid. "I like your braids," he said.

"I like your brain," I said. Oh, no. What weirdo says they like a brain?

But Johnny smiled. "That's the nicest thing anyone's ever said to me. Most people just like my eyes." **WHAT PEOPLE?** I thought.

And then we sort of looked at each other for a little too long and heard Peter say, "Ugh, let's go, this is disgusting," but it wasn't.

THEN, even though part of me wanted to throw up but in a good way (weird, I hadn't known there was a good way), Johnny said, "This was fun. I hope we can do it again soon."

"Me too!" I said. My brain said, **DO WHAT AGAIN SOON? HAVE A DATE? OR JUST GO SOMEWHERE TOGETHER AND HAVE YOU CONFUSE ME? AND WHY DID YOU STOP HOLDING MY HAND???**

But I didn't vomit.

So, basically, if you could win a first date, I totally had. Narrowly.

Final Score: Lost track due to nervous excitement— NEED THAT NEXT DATE ON THE SCHEDULE!

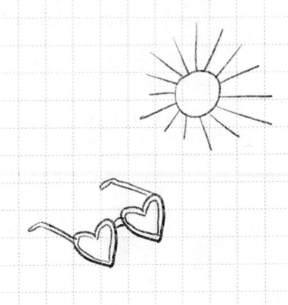

DIEGO'S TOP BIRDS OF COSTA RICA

- Two crested guan named Truman and Harlow (they are glamorous)

- A white ibis named Lou

- A bare-shanked shriek owl named Jamal

- Four green honeycreepers named Joe, Joseph, Joey, and Josephine

- A red-headed barbet who Diego did not name because it flew away with his bagel once

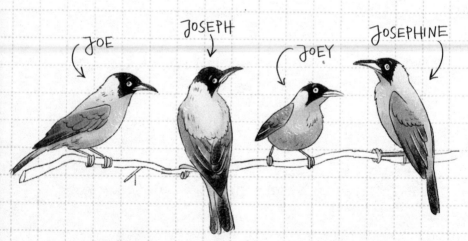

JOE   JOSEPH   JOEY   JOSEPHINE

☆4 GREEN HONEYCREEPERS

IMPORTANT UPDATE!

(June 19, later)

I have good news and bad news. Which do you want to hear first?

Oh, okay, as important as you are to me, playbook, you're never going to answer, so I guess this is up to me.

The good news is:

Diego is coming back to Peach Tree! This is an amazing seasonal development that neither of us was expecting. But we just exchanged these chats (**OLD ME**, if you're reading this and we now communicate only by holograms, just remember that every so often, Diego got to chat with me online—which is a more ancient form of cell phone texting—from an internet café in a small village wherever he is in Costa Rica).

Diego has been gone for six months—the longest we've been separated—because he moved partway through last school year.

Diego: This is exciting!

Gabby: You met another bird?

(The reason for the list of birds on the previous page is because Diego was unable to attend regular school while in the deep tropics, so he literally learned the meaning of having feathered friends. The monkeys, he told me, were not so friendly.)

Diego: No. I meet birds every day. They're exciting in a different way.

Gabby: Joe, Joey, Joseph, and Josephine seem like birds I'd get along with.

Diego: They are people-friendly. But I'm pretty sure Josephine winked at me today. She might be too attached.

Gabby: You're a likeable person. Even to birds.

Diego: I'll miss them.

Gabby: **MISS THEM?????**

Diego: **YES!** Definitely going to miss them.

Gabby: Where are they going?

Diego: Not them, **ME**.

I tried to think of what bird-free part of Costa Rica Diego would have to go to. Were there places in the world that didn't have birds?

Diego: You know . . . because I'm coming back to Peach Tree.

Gabby: What??? Why didn't you tell me sooner?

Diego: I did! Didn't you read my letter?

(Playbook, I had no idea what he was talking about but as I was trying to recall it, I saw a letter next to my computer, just under the program from Molly's graduation. I hadn't even opened it.)

To:
Gabby Garcia
2562 Broad St.
Peach Tree, GA 30312
U.S.A

Gabby: Oh, silly me! Yes, **YOUR LETTER**! About **COMING HOME**!

(Playbook, this is 100 percent a fake, like in basketball where you seem to be going up for a shot but are actually waiting for your defender to jump so you can go around him.)

Diego: Yep. It's going to be weird to be back.

Gabby: **WHY?**

Diego: I dunno. Just, jungle life I guess.

Gabby: It'll be **GREAT**.

Diego: You're probably right. I'll see you **SUPER SOON**!

So, I was lucky in a way that Diego didn't seem to notice that I'd completely missed a very nice letter—he'd even drawn a very colorful bird on the envelope. But after I read it and felt glad he was coming home, I was very bothered by it. Not by the letter, but by the fact that I'd shoved it on my desk and forgotten it.

Diego is my oldest friend, and if I had ignored his letter to me, that was like three strikes in one. Like, how bad was it that a couple days ago, I'd been loafing on the couch, feeling like I really needed him around for the summer all while his letter had been sitting there and I'd missed it because it had come when I had more to do? The game, the talent show, graduation, the talent squad party, my **DATE**, even my untethered day had all been about **ME**, while Diego's letter was sitting there ignored.

MVP Summer Gabby would never have let this happen. Even if she'd been sad about Diego, she would have been figuring out how to still have an awesome summer from afar. Now that Diego was coming back, I had to have **THAT** Gabby ready to play. From **ANEAR**!

MVP Summer Gabby would have opened that nice letter immediately and had a full plan for Diego's return. I needed to step up my game. It wasn't just my summer at stake. Having this great summer equaled a win at the **GAME OF LIFE**, too.

Okay, here I am at 4:37 p.m. on June 19, writing this down to make it official: this summer will be the MVP Summer I was destined for.

(To be continued after this dinner break . . .)

Somewhere between my first hot dog and my third one (it's hot dog night because Dad is on deadline but he still

set up a toppings bar because he's Dad and deadlines don't mean you go without avocado on your dog if that's what you really want), I told my parents about my plan.

"Diego's coming back," I said, slapping Peter's hand away as he tried to steal the last of the mango-peach salsa, even though **MY SPOON** was in the bowl. I gave everyone time to say "That's wonderful!" "What a great surprise!" "I get the last **CHEESE DOG**, then" (Peter), and then said, "And, to mark the occasion"—I wanted everyone to understand the importance of the event—"I'm planning the MVP Summer as the biggest, best summer of our lives."

"Wow," Louie said. "That sounds like a big undertaking. I'm sure Diego will just be happy to be home. Don't put too much pressure on yourself."

She must have seen my sudden frown, which was in no way linked to the delicious last spoonful of mango-peach salsa because she added, "I only mean that you might have more fun if the expectations aren't so high."

"It's Gabby we're talking about," Dad said. I didn't know exactly what that meant until he added, "I think it sounds like a heroic quest." I was about to agree but he went on to say that "deciding on a template for your deeds" (huh?) is something Don Quixote could have benefitted from. (*Don Quixote* is one of his favorite books.)

And then he chuckled and said, "Ha, imagine Don Quixote with a template." (He is really stressed right now,
so I let it go.)

BUT Don Quixote is a **HUGE BOOK**, so it did get me
thinking: Why not pack this MVP Summer with so much
FUN it could fill a book? A Don Quixote–sized book?

I had to go big, or go home.

Scratch that. I am going big, 'cause Diego's (almost)
home!

MVP SUMMER,
AN ABBREVIATED TEMPLATE OF DEEDS

- Braves game (Sundae in a ball cap will be eaten!)

- Try no less than **FIVE** new treats from the Freezemobile!

- After-dark lightning-bug bike ride

- Sugar rush pancake bar breakfast

- Terrorize Peter with scary ghost stories

- Rip Tide Water Park lazy river and lemonade lull-a-thon

- Rip Tide Water Park scary slide repeat ride scream-a-thon

- Peach Tree Summer Daze Carnival, unchaperoned, complete with goals:

  * Ride every thrill ride (Even the Zipper, which I had been avoiding since an unfortunate post-cheese fries incident on it when I was nine)

* Eat nothing but funnel cake (Because, really, unattended preteens with pocket money can't do much better for a meal, and dessert)

* Win the most obnoxious **GINORMOUS** stuffed animals available—I will do this at the milk bottle toss—which is not rigged but is very hard if you're not an excellent pitcher like me—and Diego will try at the weight-guessing booth (He is denser than he looks)

• Finally: **THE** thirteenth birthday party extravaganza!

NO-BUMMER SUMMER

MVP Summer Goal: Cook up the ultimate MVP Summer Action plan (a BBQ of ideas plus toppings!)

MVP Summer Action: Realize that summer is already **HERE** and I better get started (and maybe freak out a little)

Post-Day Analysis:
June 20

So, in the middle of my **MEGA-EXCITEMENT** about the MVP Summer, the one thing that I hadn't really thought about was how tomorrow is the first official day of it! I have no warm-up! No preseason! And can you really practice for **FUN**? I think not.

So the MVP Summer is already in play and I'm working toward the **BEST, MOST MEMORABLE, MOST AMAZING**

SUMMER of my or Diego's life, but I don't even have anything to judge it against. Weirdly, if you look at history books, they track a lot of important stuff but not really fun stuff. Like, what did Napoleon's greatest summer look like? Or Betsy Ross's? I love having guidance and role models but this quest is all mine to figure out. This might be the point where others would quit, but I **WILL NOT**.

I'll take it day by day. And when I look back on my season, I will know for sure if it was an MVP Summer or not.

MVP RANDOMNESS

2005
NEVER LEAVES
DIRTY SOCKS ON
LOCKER ROOM FLOOR

2007
ALWAYS
SHARES GUM

2011
NEVER FORGETS
A BIRTHDAY

I looked up how MVPs are chosen in baseball. (I would have asked Diego, who knows all that stuff, but I didn't want to ruin the surprise. I mean, of course he'd want to have a great, best-ever summer, but he had no idea I'd now planned an **MVP SUMMER**! He loved my plans. In fact, I was counting on him to say, "What's the plan?" so I could announce this one to great fanfare!)

I just needed to understand the factors that go into choosing a sports MVP and then translate them to a summer rating system. But what I found out happens with baseball MVPs is that two sportswriters in each city review the season, rank the most "all-around" best players in each league—American and National—and give them points for who is first-most valuable, then second-most, then third-most, and on and on. They look at stats and records and all of that, but there is no formula that says a good batting average is worth more than, say, most bases stolen or runs batted in or the lowest ERA (actually, pitchers don't win the award as often as I would have thought. **HMM** . . . seems like an opportunity!).

So what it means is, **THE JUDGES JUST CHOOSE**. If they wanted to, they could decide that a player should be MVP because his ball cap fits really well and it looks like he brushes his teeth every day. The standards could be very low.

To have an MVP Summer, you can't rely on stats or games or little things: you have to be living it **ALL THE TIME**. And there are no judges, except yourself. So my MVP Summer campaign starts immediately and **EVERY-THING COUNTS**.

Maybe instead of being like those totally random

sportswriters, I'd use a point system. Why hadn't **THEY** thought of that??

Maybe on days when I have an **MVP** Summer goal in mind, I can award myself up to 100 positive points based on how close I come (or negative points, but I doubt I'll need them). Then, by the end of August, if I have, say 1,500 points, I can consider the season an **MVP** Summer?

Bah. I wish I could just have someone tell me if I was doing a good job, like Bob and Judy.

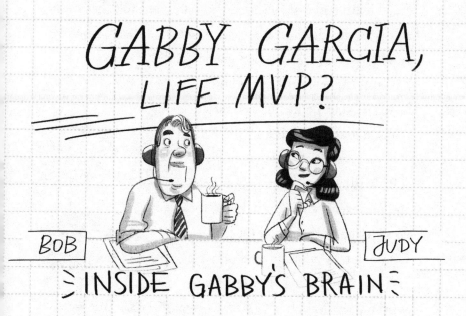

GABBY GARCIA, LIFE MVP?

BOB

JUDY

≡INSIDE GABBY'S BRAIN≡

Bob: *Gabby is really dead-set on this MVP Summer thing, Judy. Do you think we can help her out?*

Judy: *Since we're in her head, Bob, aren't we helping her out already?*

Bob: *Oh. You're right. Judy, have I told you lately that you are really a smart person?*

Judy: *We come from the same brain, Bob.*

Bob: *You're right about that!!*

Thanks a lot, Brain. I'll have to go with the points system, starting with the events of today:

Earlier, I was out with Louie having what she called a "Girls' Day." This was probably her solution to my "untethered" feeling and it wasn't a bad one but I told her every day is a girls' day and a boys' day and shouldn't we be past labels by now? She seemed encouraged by my "zing" (her word) and admitted I raised a good point but also that I might understand later.

We went to get pedicures, which I'll admit, once I got past the "my feet are too ticklish for this!" issue, was kind of nice, 'cause I do a lot of running and standing and stuff, so sitting in a big chair with my feet in bub- bly warm water

and then having them scrubbed with yummy smelling stuff . . . it wasn't as weird as I imagined.

Louie definitely didn't think it was weird. Because one second she was reading a celebrity magazine and the next she was almost snoring. And her snoring, instead of being disturbing, was kind of relaxing. I leaned my big chair back and closed my eyes and envisioned a candy-coated world where everything smelled as good as the sugar scrub that was all over my feet but also you could eat the candy because no one had ever put it on anyone's feet. Now **THAT** would have been an MVP Summer highlight. I had my dream list of deeds but I needed some extra stuff. Cookouts were good. My dad could help with the food part but maybe I could make some awesome cake decked out in the entire rainbow of candy. Should we have a lemonade stand? No, better to just be the awesome big kids buying lemonade from little kids. We could probably hike to Peach Tree Point, one of the highest spots in Georgia. But I needed even bigger things, didn't I? I couldn't stop thinking about **SKYDIVING**! Or sneaking in to a concert and **WINDING UP ON STAGE**! Or maybe throwing out an opening pitch at a Braves game. (Really, I can't believe they've never asked me.)

Just as my imagination steered me to riding my bike so fast that flames shot out the back while Diego skateboarded next to me with a Popsicle in each hand, the lady sugar-coating my toes started asking me where I went to school. Who asked that on the almost-first day of summer???

I snapped out of my daydream and stumbled around for an answer. Stumbled around in my brain. The pedicure lady was still holding my feet and they were unavailable for stumbling.

"Um, well, I went to Piper Bell. Last year. But before that, Luther."

"Is that the one they closed for the asbestos?"

I nodded. "Yup. That's why I went to Piper Bell. But now it's reopened. And in the fall, I'll be going to Luther again."

"Oh, that's a lot of change for you," the pedicurist said. "Unless you hated Piper Bell. In which case, good riddance, right?"

"Uh, sure," I said. "Luther is my home school. But Piper Bell was great. *Is* great."

That was true. I had really liked it, with its perfect baseball fields and the atrium and the talent squad. I think I liked it even better because I went there thinking I wouldn't fit, and then I had. Luther had French Fry Fridays and everyone I had grown up with and I could walk there with Diego, but I was worried that someday Piper Bell would feel like it had never happened. These thoughts were not the ideal interruption to my MVP Summer mission.

Louie had woken up and was listening to me, which sort of made me more nervous because when she and Dad told me about the very small chance for a Piper Bell scholarship, I knew they felt bad because it was too expensive to just enroll me. But with Diego back, it's not like I'd abandon him anyway. He'd been in the jungle for months, away from everything. And after our MVP Summer, we'd be inseparable again. It would be bonkers to even consider going to different schools.

"The school did mention a chance of a scholarship," Louie said, and she sounded proud. "But it will mean someone else turns one down, so fingers crossed." She was wide awake after her snorefest and she looked at me and smiled, like she was trying to apologize but was also hopeful the scholarship would work out.

Don Quixote probably just got to do his quest without all these side questions. So much for a relaxing Girls' Day!

"Well, she can't cross her fingers if I'm going to paint her nails," the pedicurist said. "So just relax."

That sounded like a good idea, so I tried, even though now that she'd brought up school, other unwelcome thoughts intruded. What if it rained all summer? Or there was a nationwide ice cream shortage? Or Diego forgot how to ride a bike?

I needed to get out of this manicure place and to the drawing board. I didn't have much time left!

But it was hard to turn down Louie when she insisted on taking me for frozen yogurt afterward at Swirl World. (Note to **OLD ME**, even though it's good, frozen yogurt will never be ice cream, which is why they need to offer people four thousand candies and toppings to put on it.) Once we'd filled our cups and got a table, Louie pushed a box across the table to me. Just a plain brown box, maybe big enough for a mouse to make a cozy-but-windowless home. I hoped it wasn't a mouse. Koufax would see to it that a mouse didn't last long. (That sounds mean, but it's just a fact.)

"What is this?" I said.

"Open it."

I did. And it was a phone. I am almost thirteen. I am supposed to have been begging for a phone now for at least the last couple of years.

But here's the key! I never begged. It was an **EXTRA-ORDINARY REVERSE PSYCHOLOGY PLAY**. If I had seemed desperate for a phone, my parents would have feared I'd turn into a phone addict.

"You look exactly the opposite of what I was expecting," Louie said, taking a spoonful of her mango yogurt.

(No toppings, because she said she likes to really taste the yogurt and yes, she is the weirdest person on the planet for that.) "I know it's not the latest model, but we got a refurbished one and . . ."

"No, this is perfect." It was, but after years of not asking for a phone, having one just handed to me totally threw me off. If I acted too excited, all the work I'd done to prove I could handle a phone without turning into a screen-drooling zombie would be for nothing.

"We feel like you're showing you can make good choices," Louie said. I didn't know about **THAT**. Had she seen the nail polish I picked for my toes? (It was dark green. When we left the nail place, I thought it was unique and cool but looking at it now, as I write this, I think it might look like my toes are growing moss.)

I got up and gave her a hug and a big smile that I hoped looked like a **GOOD-CHOICES GRIN** and not a **GONNA-SCREW-THIS-UP SMIRK**.

"I spoke to Diego's

mom. He'll have one, too. We thought since you'll be getting more independent and busier, it will be a good way for us to be able to get ahold of you when we need to."

Independent! Busy! "This is going to make the MVP Summer even **BETTER**!" I mean, really, after months of hardly being able to communicate, now Diego and I could be communicating **ALL THE TIME**! About **FUN THINGS**.

Louie frowned. Uh-oh. Had I gotten too excited about my new technology? "Just be reasonable," she said. "And if you screw up, just own your screwup."

I nodded like that made any sense. Who would want to **OWN A SCREWUP**?

"Absolutely, sure thing, I'll own them all!" I said, just

ME &
MY SCREWUPS
SHOW...

to avoid the discussion because I really wanted to take my phone out of the box.

I did and pressed the power button and—**IT WAS SO SHINY**! Like a trophy! That makes phone calls! And takes pictures! And sends texts!

To avoid those screwups I don't want to own, here are a few rules I'm going to try:

1. No texting to someone who is in the room with me.
2. If I am with a friend, don't text or stare at phone much. **RUDE!**
3. Don't take pictures of **EVERYTHING**, but definitely try not to miss any **AMAZING SHOTS!**
4. Don't ever say things like, "My phone is the most important thing in my life."
5. Totally make my little brother, Peter, jealous that I have a phone and he doesn't. (I'm only human.)
6. Also, learn emoji. (They are too cute to avoid.)

MVP Summer Points: 50 points for plans in the works and a heart emoji in the right place!

MVP Summer Tally: 50

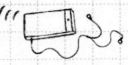

FOUL BALL

MVP Summer Goal: Have a first day of summer that sets the bar for the whole **SEASON**!

MVP Summer Action: Play all-star baseball. It's almost too easy!

Post-Day Analysis:
June 21

It was the first **DAY OF SUMMER**! (Well, technically, it still is, but it's night now.) And my first day of MVP Summer was taking place on a baseball field!

Today, I was about to start as a pitcher for the Peach Tree All-Star Team—the **INAUGURAL** one. Inaugural means **FIRST-EVER** and **I LOVE GOING FIRST**!

Plus, the added bonus: the other players are people I

already know and like: a few kids I played with at Luther, plus Devon DeWitt, Ryder Mills, and Mario Salamida, who were on the team at Piper Bell.

We're so good that we get to have two coaches! Coach Daniels, from Luther, and Coach Hollylighter, from Piper Bell. It's true that Coach Hollylighter and I didn't exactly hit it off on the right foot but Coach Daniels **LOVES** me. When I played for him at Luther, I was the Golden Child. I know, I know, I'm not necessarily trying to be the favorite or the best or to get special treatment, but with Coach Daniels, I don't have to try. It just **HAPPENS**. I figure with him around, it will balance Coach Hollylighter, who is pretty tough. (Even Devon agrees, and Devon is so tough I've seen her catch a ball barehanded like it was a marshmallow.)

Coach Hollylighter was late. **THAT** was weird. I asked Devon and Mario about it. "Hollylighter being late is like the sun deciding not to rise, or be hot," Mario said. Devon looked up at the sun then, to check if it was still there, and then blinked a few times. (It has nothing to do with the sun, just something she does when she's thinking.)

"If she's not here in fifteen minutes, we should probably alert the authorities," Devon agreed. But Coach Daniels was ready to go and went through the roster. Devon and I would be the go-to pitchers. "I know Garcia pretty

well," Coach Dan-
iels told everyone.
"She has a text-
book example of a
great pitching arm,
except the poor bat-
ters don't get to read
the textbook before
they come up against
her."

Can I blame myself
for feeling pretty awesome about that? I think not.

He had us warm up and do introductions with a round
of catch where we said our name as a way of learning who
we all were.

"Gabby!" I said, tossing it to Casey Allen, a boy who'd
played Little League with me and was on the Luther team.

"Casey!" he yelled, lobbing it at Mario.

"Mario," he bellowed, because he always bellows, and
tossed it to Devon, who said, "Devon," with her usual
glinty-eyed cowboy face (Devon was **VERY** hard to read)
as she hurled it to Alfonso Juego, who'd gone to Luther
with me.

When we'd done that for a few rounds, Coach Daniels
let me take the mound, and he scattered a few players in

the field so everyone could get used to working together as a team. One thing I noticed was different about Coach Daniels than Coach Hollylighter is that no matter what kind of pitch I threw, he thought it was great.

Coach Hollylighter had always been pointing out things about my form, like telling me when my arm was just a little too bent on the throw, or when I needed to be looser—"going gummy," she called it, because that was when my curves were curviest.

Not Coach Daniels:

"Amazing slider, Garcia! Look at that, team!"

"That had to be a hundred-mile-per-hour fastball!" (It wasn't. I'm only twelve! Getting sixty miles per hour is huge.)

"I can't believe anyone can hit that curve!"

This all felt great. Total MVP Summer–caliber praise. But I was starting to get a little worried about Coach Hollylighter.

"Are you sure you told Coach Hollylighter the right field?" I asked Coach Daniels.

He nodded. "She picked the field," he said. "To be honest, she's the one really running the show here. If she's late, she had a good reason."

I caught Devon's eye as she sat in the dugout and she gave a little nod, like this made sense to her. Then Coach

Daniels said it was Devon's turn on the mound.

As she jogged out to take over for me, we heard Coach Hollylighter's voice.

"I see you got started without me," she said. If she'd gotten there just two minutes earlier, she'd have witnessed at least some of Coach Daniels's Golden Child praise.

But I'd be pitching all season. She'd hear it eventually.

Or I thought she would. But then Coach Hollylighter walked out to the mound and said this: "Actually, Gabby and Devon won't be pitching this season."

"Huh?" I said.

"What?" Devon said. It was pretty easy to read her at that moment: she was **NOT** happy about this.

Coach Daniels would put a stop to this. Devon and I

turned and looked at him. But then he slapped his fore-head. "Oh, that's right! I'll let Coach explain." *But you're a coach, too!* I thought.

"We're trying something unconventional this season," Coach Hollylighter said. "Everyone is going to play new positions."

But my arm is **TEXTBOOK**! Textbooks know things! Why would you mess with that? It didn't make any sense.

"I know some of you are thinking this doesn't make any sense," she said, as if she'd read my mind. Sometimes I was scared she could do that. "You're young players and even though you're each very good at what you do, this is a sea-son for teaching you to be adaptable and to get out of your comfort zone."

"What's wrong with comfort zones?" Devon said to me under her breath about one second before I said the exact same thing.

She was 100 percent right. What was the point of practicing and playing pitcher all your life? To get **COM-FORTABLE** at it.

We weren't the only ones who felt that way. Every-one was moaning and groaning. Mario kicked the dirt and said, "We'll lose every game. We'll never get a trophy."

"I think you're overreacting," Coach Hollylighter said. "First off, we're not even sure there IS a trophy yet. This all-star league is new. We're still working on that."

"What?" I blurted. "This is the worst."

"Look, you can play because you love the game or because you get a prize. I think you know where you stand, Garcia," Coach H. said. She had me there.

"Okay, but I just love the game more when I'm pitching!"

"Believe it or not, the Chicago Cubs worked this same kind of position switcheroo in 2016."

I had two immediate thoughts: (1.) Coach Hollylighter saying the word "switcheroo" in her very serious voice was really kind of funny. (2.) Before 2016, anyone saying "the Cubs did this" would have been laughed at, since the team hadn't won a World Series in 108 years. But in 2016, they DID. And it was a pretty awesome season, and series.

"So, if pros can try it, I think All-Star Little Leaguers should try it, too. Now, let's start you at your new positions."

She read off a roster of where we were each going to play. Mario was going to take over third base, which didn't seem like that big a stretch from first, even if he'd see less action; and Devon would be playing shortstop. Casey Allen and Alfonso, who'd both been at Luther with me, were going to take over as pitchers.

"Garcia, get a mask on; you're catcher," Coach said.

Catcher? Ugh. I didn't want to be catcher. Look, I can

write this here because it's a personal and private playbook but catcher is a fine position, a great position, as long as one thing is true: you're the pitcher.

I can appreciate a good catcher. I **NEED** a good catcher. But when you can play pitcher, you're the center of the game. Why would I want to give that up?

The only thing was, I knew Coach Hollylighter well enough by now to know that she wouldn't give me what I wanted just because I thought she should. So I'd have to play her way and put all my energy into hoping she'd come to her senses.

As I write this, I worry that having to play the wrong position isn't exactly the formula for an MVP Summer. But neither is moping about playing the wrong position. And at least behind a catcher's mask, I could scowl all I wanted without anyone noticing.

MVP Summer Points: A full 100 because I kept my cool, even if this feels like a great big 0

MVP Summer Tally: 150, but catcher? REALLY?

MANY HAPPY RETURNS

MVP Summer Goal: Get psyched for the MVP Summer by filling in Katy on my plans

MVP Summer Action: Make sure my summer plans have excellent word of mouth (easy, since it's **MY MOUTH**!)

Post-Day Analysis:
June 22

I didn't start today with my goal and strategy mapped out. I started today trying to plan an amazing summer that Diego would never forget but that also figured in how I have new things in my life that might come into play. Like Johnny. And the all-star team. And my new Piper Bell friends. I wasn't sure I could have an MVP Summer without including all of them but **DIEGO** had to be the **MOST IMPORTANT** summer co-winner.

Ping! I got a text. From Katy Harris. I get texts now! Or, well, a text. (I'd drafted a text to Johnny. It said, "Hi! Happy summer!" But then I couldn't decide between a winky smiley face—did that mean I didn't mean what I said? But was the regular smiley face too serious in a way? So I sent a sunshine emoji and an ice cream cone. Genius! Except he'd sent back a **WINKY FACE**. What did it **MEAN**?)

KATY
(AKA BABY BEYONCÉ)

FIERCE, CONFIDENT ATTITUDE

"SUPER" SINGING VOICE

♪ ♫ AWESOME DANCE MOVES

✦SPARKLY✦ BUT NOT TO BE MESSED WITH

Katy was probably the person on the talent squad I got closest with at Piper Bell. I'm still getting the feel for being her friend, because she's sort of a celebrity. She may be the biggest talent of the talent squad, as she is basically a Baby Beyoncé.

Here's what it said (being the first text I had ever got, it seems like the thing to do).

Katy: Hey, GG! Wanna hang? I am songwtg.

(I need to get better at abbreviations in my new phone/texting world.)

Gabby: YES!

It was kind of exciting, getting a text from Katy. It was also kind of a relief to get it when I did, because instead of panicking about my MVP Summer approach, I had a distraction. Like **PING**! Take your mind off a tricky subject with this handy interruption. Kind of like when you go to a Major League game in person and your team is losing, so you're flipping out a little but then, on the scoreboard, three donuts are in a race and it becomes the most important thing you can think of. No matter how down you are, you turn and look at the scoreboard and pick a donut and watch it run, or roll, depending on whether whoever made up the race for that day thinks donuts get around on skinny little legs or just by their natural circular-ness.

Distractions are nice.

And I did tell Katy that I wanted to keep doing the poetry thing. Because I've decided that even though at the time it was a diversion from my real dream of baseball, I also figured out that I really like writing. Many of the best athletes also have other hobbies and interests, so I think it's important I do, too.

DONUTS AS DISTRACTIONS
(WHAT'S NOT TO LOVE?)

OTHER INTERESTS OF PRO ATHLETES

- **David Beckham**, pro soccer player, likes fencing.

- **Serena Williams**, pro tennis superstar, is a fashion genius.

- **Rajon Rondo**, pro basketball player, is constantly roller skating.

- **Tim Duncan**, pro basketball player, also plays Dungeons and Dragons.

- **Mo'ne Davis**, Little League baseball player, loves to play basketball.

- **Muhammad Ali**, pro boxer, considered the Greatest of All Time, was kind of a poet, like me ("float like a butterfly, sting like a bee"—that was him just **TALKING**!).

So, I changed gears and went to Katy's house. Katy's room is more than just a bedroom. It's a STUDIO. (In all honesty, it wasn't that much bigger than my bedroom but, as Katy explained, she is all about "positive visualization.")

When I got there, she had a chair for me at her "song-writing station." It looked like just a desk from IKEA but since she had the name for it, it suddenly became just what she said: **A STATION**. For songwriting. Above it was what she called a "gallery wall" with framed inspirational quotes and photos from her performances and all kinds of pictures and artwork of places she had been and wants to go. (Been: New York City, Los Angeles, Nashville. Wants to Go: Paris, Tokyo, Spain.)

So then it came to me: Katy would know exactly how to have an over-the-top summer! And if she liked the ideas, of course Diego would.

She poured me a glass of icy lemonade from a glass pitcher—what eighth-grader-to-be had their own beautiful glass pitcher?—and said, "Okay, what are you feeling today?"

And right away, because she asked the question, I said, "Unsure."

"Well, there's your poetic theme for now. I'm writing about getting big."

I didn't understand what she meant, so I asked, "Like

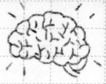

growing up? Like your career when you're big?"

Katy thoughtfully bit the end of her pen. "No, like after the talent show, I keep getting asked to perform new places, and it's everything I wanted but also it's scary," she said. "Because I don't want who I am to change. And I don't want to disappoint anyone. I just want to have a normal summer that's, like, also not plain ol' normal."

The "**WHOA**" lights in my brain went off. Because Katy had just said almost exactly what my "unsure" meant. I wanted everything about this summer to be the same, but also better than the same, and also different. How could I not be unsure, with a goal like that?

"Do you think if you ate cherry Popsicles every day for the summer, you would have a permanently bright red tongue? Do you like lazy rivers or superfast water slides? Have you ever tried riding your bike down Tangerine Overlook? Is it true that you have to fall to stop? How tall do you have to be to skydive?"

Katy was holding her lemonade glass in midair, just looking at me. I guess that was a fair reaction to someone bombarding you with a series of questions out of nowhere. "Wait, what's going on, GG?"

I shrugged and told her about Diego coming home and how I wanted to get the MVP Summer off to the ideal start and have the rest of it planned **PERFECTLY**. "I need to make this summer the best MVP Summer it can be," I said. If Katy gave some of my ideas the seal of approval, then they had to be can't-miss, right?

"I don't know what you're worried about," she said. "You always seem to have a plan for everything." She thought that? Maybe my playbook life is really working. Or maybe everyone went around thinking everyone else knew what they were doing but no one really did. No, it was probably the playbook.

I was feeling pretty proud of myself until she added, "But maybe you shouldn't be too plan-y now."

"I don't get it," I said.

"An MVP Summer is, like, what, just nonstop fun and adventure or something?"

"Yup. Imagine the perfect summer day and then put three of those days into one summer day."

"You don't think that seems a little . . . high pressure?" Katy said this in a calm way, like she was just curious, not really doubting the MVP Summer. She sounded kind of like Louie.

I scribbled a phrase in my notebook and showed it to her. "Have you heard of this saying? 'Shoot for the moon. If you miss you'll still be among the stars'?"

Katy nodded. "It's on like every teachers' bulletin board everywhere, isn't it?"

"Sure," I said, now crossing things out. "Well, MVP Summer is shoot for ice cream sundaes all the time. If you miss, you'll still have a Popsicle."

Katy had to understand that. Or maybe she was lactose intolerant and preferred Popsicles anyway. She paced her room. "I think it's okay if your summer is even more chill than that," she said. "If Diego is coming back, maybe that's a big enough deal. He doesn't need anything over the top."

Sigh. I wasn't sure she was getting it. Katy was great, but making new friends is a bit like throwing a first pitch with a brand-new baseball: you have to get a feel for it before you're sure what to do with it. Diego would love if the summer was over the top.

Like, sure, Diego **COULD** just come home and everything could be exactly like any other kid's summer but the MVP Summer was **INSPIRING**. And I knew he'd feel the same way. We fit in each other's life like a glove. Ha!

YOU'RE TOO NEW!

"Maybe you're right," I said to Katy, kind of fibbing.

She would understand the MVP Summer once she witnessed it. I bet a lot of people didn't understand *Don Quixote*, either. (Note to self: I should really read that book someday.)

But since she and Louie had said the same thing about the pressure and expectations, I had an idea: I wouldn't **TELL** Diego we were living the MVP Summer until it was clearly under way. In baseball, players get to rack up a bunch of great games before anyone says, "You're in the running for MVP." Starting out the summer **KNOWING** you had to make it an MVP one might make you nervous.

The summer would be like that—in the middle of something **SUPER FUN**, I would ask Diego, "So, how about this MVP Summer we're having???" It would be like the excellent fastball I threw just when I needed it. I had to pick my moment.

"I know I'm right," Katy said, snapping me out of my planning. "You're like a **LIFE MVP**."

That was the nicest thing anyone ever said to me. "I wish a person could be that. A Most Valuable Person."

"I love that. Most Valuable Person. We should write a song about **THAT**," Katy said.

What? Katy wanted to write a song with me?? It was another distraction, because my stomach had started getting knotty wondering about the skydiving thing.

So we set to work. First we brainstormed key words.

LIST OF KEY WORDS

Katy told me that word association was a good way to get your brain moving, like warming up for a game. And then we came up with a chorus. I don't know if it was working in a studio or at a songwriting station or what but Katy and I were just doing awesome together. I would say something smart and then she'd add to it and then we'd rhyme it and **BLAMMO**!

> "I wanna be bigger than me
> Most Valuable Person
> An MVP
> It's not for the glory, it's not for the fame
> But so you think good things when you hear my name."

We sang that part together after Katy set it to a beat

she programmed into her computer.

"I've never had such a cool collaborator before," Katy said, beaming. "Let's work on the first verse."

"I was thinking something like, 'It's not easy, trying to get this life thing right,'" I said, because it was totally what I was feeling. Except about the summer.

We kept writing for a while, and after an hour we didn't have a whole song but we had some good verses. And when Katy and I high-fived our progress, I felt the slightest bit guilty: I hadn't thought about the summer or Diego that whole time.

"You really meant what you said, about the planning?" I asked Katy. "It's just, Diego missed a lot. I don't want him to feel left out of my new life."

"Easy-peasy, MVP-sy." Katy smiled and scribbled that down. "You'll know what to do once you see him. Things sometimes seem strange or a little bit blurry, but time fixes lots, so you don't have to hurry."

"Write that down," I said. And then I did, too.

MVP Summer Points: Out of 100 possible points, a solid 80 because I was waiting for my moment

MVP Summer Tally: 230 with MANY MORE TO COME

A TRIP DOWN MEMORY LANE

MVP Summer Goal: Welcome Diego back with the ultimate catch-up session
MVP Summer Action: Focus on everything he missed while he was gone

Post-Day Analysis:
June 23

Diego's home! He landed late last night and the whole family was exhausted due to some travel delays, so I haven't seen him yet but tomorrow night we are going to have one of our **EPIC SLEEPOVERS**.

When Diego said it was going to be weird to be back, I didn't know what exactly that would mean. I decided the first action I needed to take was to catch him up on what he missed in Peach Tree. So I made stations for each month he was gone.

December: Xmas cookies, sing fave songs

January: New Year Celebration! Confetti, party horns, countdown to a new year!

February: Fake snow station to reenact the random storm we had late in the month

March: Spring Training! Recap fave player moves and stats, make predictions for who will be tops by All-Star break (sort of unfair, since the break is nearly here but we can pretend it's not)

April: Opening Day! Baseball foodfest: hot dogs, ice cream, popcorn

May/June: End of school/start of summer mini dance party (a Garcia–Parker tradition)

Basically, each station will be helpful as Diego re-assimilates to Peach Tree life. He won't feel weird. He'll feel like he never really left. (Re-assimilate is another one of my dad's words that means, more or less, helping someone get back to their normal life. So, hmm, it's like this movie my dad likes with Tom Hanks in it, and he's a delivery man or something and he gets stranded on this tropical island by himself and ends up talking to a volleyball. That's about as much of it as I can explain because it's very much a dad movie and I think he secretly likes it because he's always wanted a beard and Louie said no way to a beard which is good because in the movie Tom Hanks's beard is scary. But anyway, Diego was like that, except beardless and talking to birds instead of a volleyball. And I have to step in to help him feel normal again.)

So, Diego coming home means we should just get right back into Best Friend mode. It's perfect, actually.

I figure by the time we get to February on my Catch You Up stations, Diego might have

I'LL HELP YOU!

regained so much lost time, he'll forget he was ever in Costa Rica in the first place. And eventually I'd spring the MVP Summer on him and any weirdness would disappear.

I was helping my dad with the Christmas cookies in the kitchen. We'd cut them all out but it was decorating time, which was my specialty. As Louie said, "I can always tell which cookies you decorated because they have too much frosting and too many sprinkles but everything is overdone in exactly the right amounts." Even though it was just me and Diego having the sleepover, we had made enough cookies for all of the Atlanta Braves, at least. And maybe the visiting team. It was a kitchen disaster because even though my dad cooks a lot, he is bad at doing it in a nice, neat, or orderly way. And today, his mind must have been on his work project because he was even messier than usual.

Peter sauntered into the kitchen and tried to take a snowman I'd frosted so it looked like it was wearing a baseball hat. (It wasn't perfect but the effort was solid.) I blocked Peter and gave him a plate of broken cookies that weren't good enough for Diego. "Why is there fake snow and confetti and party horns and All-Star ballots spread out on the dining room table?" He chomped on a broken reindeer. "And why am I eating Christmas cookies?"

"Diego's Peach Tree Catch-Up Stations. There's an activity for every month he was gone."

Peter snort-laughed. "Ugh. Sounds like someone is trying too hard."

"Thank you," I said. Because if Peter thought I was trying too hard, it had to mean I was trying just the right amount. Tomorrow was going to be **PERFECT**!

MVP Summer Points: 100 Points for TRYING TOO HARD (aka just hard enough)

 ## MVP Summer Tally: 330

THE ARRIVAL
TIME-OUT! EMERGENCY
SLEEPOVER ENTRY

Night of June 24

Okay, this is weird, but you know how I said I was going to help Diego catch up and feel exactly like things are the same?? Well, I'm sitting here in the bathroom writing this down because Diego has thrown me a curve.

'Cause he's totally different!

He has a shell necklace (this probably sounds like a not-big deal because it's just a necklace but Diego is someone who avoids accessories at all costs because they lead to mishaps. Like, the one time we tried to wear matching friendship bracelets, his got stuck on a tree branch and he sprained his wrist).

He's super tan.

His hair is pretty long. No beard though, so that's a good thing.

I think he got taller. But he always gets taller, so in that way, he's the same?

He usually sprinkles all his conversation with sports facts but now he's talking about birds. A lot. You would think the birds are Major League Baseball players, he knows so much about each one of them. For example, the keel-billed toucan's beak is more than just beautiful, it's helpful for picking berries! The blue-crowned motmot has to be observed from a shadowy distance near wetlands because it eats frogs. The blue-gray tanager is hard to watch for long

SEEMS TALLER ↓

SHELL NECKLACE ?? 🐚 ??

WEARS BINOCULARS... 👁 👁

TROPICAL MOTIFS

WHO IS THIS PERSON ??

REALLY TANNED ☀

because it's speedy and restless. I was getting restless wondering when he'd stop showing me bird photos!

And, with the stations, well, he was amused by them but not as **EXCITED** as I'd thought he'd be. Like, instead of having the fake snowball fight I'd planned, he started wondering about how the Atlanta bird population had fared during the winter.

And, more generally, he **SEEMS** different. I can't quite explain how.

♪ ♫
SLEEP ON IT

MVP Summer Goal: Bend space and time so that it's like Diego never left and hopefully have a moment when the MVP Summer can officially be announced!

MVP Summer Action: Be ready for Diego to ask, "What's the plan?"

Post-Day Analysis:
June 24

"This makes no sense!" I yelled at the TV. "After dinosaurs almost eat people at your theme park three times, why would you keep it open? This makes no sense!"

Diego and I were watching *Jurassic World*. His pick. I let him choose because I was feeling too down about his kind of **MEH** reaction to the stations. I shouldn't say **MEH** because he was smiling and impressed but then he said, "I thought we could just watch a movie."

And I thought to myself, *I thought you would be up for my* **AMAZING MONTHLY MEMORY-MAKING STATIONS**. But he had eaten several cookies, at least. And popcorn. And a hot dog. And then said we should order a pizza from Peace-a-Pizza, his favorite place. And when I asked if he hadn't eaten in the jungle, he said he was a growing boy, so at least that explains the height thing.

"Scientific discovery can't always make sense right away!" Diego chimed in, digging into our bucket of popcorn searching for the M&M's we'd mixed in that had fallen to the bottom. So, okay, it wasn't the worst, not doing my stations. This was fun.

"Well, I, for one, think someone should call the Better Business Bureau on them."

"Velociraptors would eat the Better Business Bureau."

"I wish they'd eat both of you guys," Peter muttered from his spot on the couch. But even he was grinning. I could tell he was happy Diego was back, too. If only because then he had two of us to make fun of.

"Did you know that really, velociraptors and many dinosaurs, in fact, had feathers, and are closely related to birds?" Oh, gosh, it was the bird thing again.

"The Toronto Raptors don't have feathers," I said,

naming the basketball team because I was trying to bring things back to sports, like a test, I suppose.

"Well, that's true, but I think they had to make them mascot-y," Diego said. "Dunking would be harder if you had giant feathers getting in the way."

We all burst out into giggles and I didn't even tell Peter to go away. It was still bothering me that I couldn't get Diego to talk about baseball at all. But we are going to the Braves game tomorrow. And, writing this now, even though I am up even later than Diego, I suppose it's okay we didn't do anything extra special. Maybe to him, since we hadn't been in the same country together for months, all the regular stuff we always did *felt* extra special.

So, we'd feasted on pizza, Diego had taught my family some birdcalls (I wondered when the bird stuff would start to wear off), we'd caught and released some fireflies as the sun was starting to go down, plus played cookie checkers (where you use cookies as your game pieces and can eat them when you take your opponent's pieces—I thought of that years ago), and then we'd watched the movie. It was midnight and I was tired and full and really happy.

"Peter!" Louie called from upstairs. "It's time for you to go to bed. We have the baseball game tomorrow."

"Aw, why does Gabby get to stay up later?"

"Because she's older."

"That's not fair. We're almost the same height."

"Peter! Bed! **NOW!**"

Peter slunk off the couch in full grumble mode. Diego rolled out his sleeping bag on the living room floor and I zipped up into mine. And from there, maybe because the movie was over and it was quiet, things started to go wrong.

"It's good to be back, Gabs," Diego said.

"I'm glad to have you back, D," I said, feeling a little shy about saying it. I'm not always good at feelings stuff. That might be why I like poetry, because it gives me a way to say it. It might also be why I like sports, because they are full of feeling but you put those feelings into actions. I'm only good at writing about them here because they are part of a playbook. And also **TOP SECRET**.

But, because it was quiet and calm, and because Diego had started a feelings talk, I didn't know what to say. "So, you really liked the jungle, then?" I asked. I tried to remember if I'd ever really asked him about it before. He'd told me things—about the crazy monkeys and the sticky hot weather and the rain that made the sticky hot weather go away—but I hadn't ever said, "So do you like it there?"

I should have asked.

"It was great," he said. "I think I might go back some-day, if I become an ornithologist."

"An orni-what-ogist???"

"It's a scientist who studies birds," he said. "I mean, I could go there, or there are amazing species in India and throughout Asia. The possibilities are only limited by where the birds are, and they're everywhere."

"I thought you wanted to be a sportswriter," I said. "That's what you always said, anyway." Part of our hoped-for plan was that maybe one day I'd be a major athlete and Diego would be a sportswriter who got to cover some of my games. And it would be a lifelong friendship that would be featured in the ESPN documentary on our lives.

"Well, nothing is for sure. I just really like birds, and studying them. It's kind of like a sport in a way," he said. "I mean, birds are nature's athletes. The things they can do while flying alone are enough to fill a million trading cards."

What? I racked my brain, trying to imag-ine how bird studies could be anything

ATHLETIC BIRD

HEADBAND

REHYDRATION

POST WORK-OUT SWEAT

LEG WARMERS

like a sport. And aren't *athletes* nature's athletes? Fortunately, before I could question his theory, Diego kept talking.

"But I am writing for the *Peach Tree Gazette* this summer!" he said. "I sent an application for its junior reporter program from Costa Rica and they picked me."

"That's great!" I said, and I meant it, because (A.) I was happy for him and (B.) maybe writing for the paper would remind him of his true sportswriting dream. "Are you doing sports?"

"Some. I was going to ask to cover the All-Stars," he said, and looked at me hopefully.

"Ugh, I'm playing catcher," I told him. I couldn't believe we'd hung out all night and I hadn't yet complained about this. "It's a long story. But maybe if you write about how good a pitcher the team is missing out on, I can play my real position."

Diego grinned. "Maybe. I was also thinking I could ask to write a birding column."

"Birding?"

"It's short for bird-watching. All the die-hard birders say it."

Oh, no. The birding thing had really gone on too long. And he considered himself "die-hard." I kept waiting for Diego to say he was joking but the more he got excited over birds, the more worried I was that he'd never feel back to normal. Also, there was the very real fact that birding is very strange and, okay, pretty uncool. One of my MVP Summer goals had to be making sure he didn't head down a wrong path in life. Birding might be fine for Diego once he was, like, eight million years old and a retired sportswriter. By then he'd have lots of respect and credibility.

But taking up a strange old-people hobby when you're turning thirteen?

It seemed to me like certain doom. Having an old-person hobby was like a force-out for all potential of cool teen years. (**OLD ME**, who has surely for-

gotten some important things, a force-out is when you're on first base and you have to run to second because someone's gotten a hit, even if that hit is sure to get you tagged out. There's no

DIEGO WALKING INTO CERTAIN DOOM !!!

{TAG OUT!}

other option. So, taking up a weird old-person hobby—don't be offended, **OLD ME**!—was like a ball hit right to second base: your out-ness was inevitable.)

How do you gently tell your friend that their new beloved pastime is certain doom? I'd just have to make the MVP Summer so good he forgot about it.

"Did you see that the Ice House closed?" Diego said, changing the subject again. At least this was very Diego: a conversation with him often covered a zillion different topics because he's so enthusiastic about facts he's learned. Those facts used to lean to the sporting ones, though, not birds. Anyway, the Ice House is—**WAS**—our favorite place for snow cones because they somehow had a million flavors lined up like a sugary rainbow behind the counter. And you could mix them, so actually, it might have had infinite flavors. Maybe that was why they couldn't stay in business. Flavor management is probably hard.

"I know, I was so bummed," I said. "The family moved to California and took all the snow cone stuff with them."

"California is lucky. And I bet they don't even appreciate all the snow cone flavors," Diego said. Then he sat up in his sleeping bag. "Coming back is strange. It's just this feeling I have, from being away. Like little things have changed on me and what did I miss?"

I gulped back what I thought about saying, which was,

"What about all the ways *you* changed? You go **BIRDING** now?!" I could feel all my little Gabbys, who usually only spring up when something really makes me nervous, starting to bound around under my skin. The little Gabbys wanted to feel settled and normal and they wanted it **NOW**. Several of them were just fidgeting and another was shoving massive amounts of popcorn in her mouth (shoving whatever food is available into my mouth is something I actually do when I'm nervous and don't know what to say). One was pretending to sleep. And that seemed like a pretty good idea.

"Gabby?" Diego asked. "Are you okay?" He must have noticed I was thinking.

"LITTLE GABBYS"

TALK NOW!

NO, WAIT!!

"Yeah, yeah, fine." I really wanted to yawn at that moment so I could blame my sudden strange behavior on being tired. But of course, you can never yawn when you'd like to yawn. "Don't worry, I think things will start to feel like home again for you soon."

Yawn, I thought. Nothing happened.

Well, when you can't force a yawn, you can smile and pretend like nothing's changed.

So I did.

MVP Summer Points: 100 points for rolling with Diego's idea of an excellent sleepover. But minus 20 points for falling asleep on a low note.

MVP Summer Tally: 410 points

IMPROVING BOARD GAMES WITH SNACK FOODS

- **Clue**—Include a "death by chocolate" option (example: It was Colonel Mustard in the Study with the Chocolate Wrench . . . hmm, chocolate murder weapons may have to be symbolic)

- **Hungry Hungry Hippos**—Use Whoppers—whatever your hippo eats, so do you!

- **Battleship**—Battle**CHIP**! Every hit gets a handful of chips (chocolate or potato)

- **Trivial Pursuit**—As you earn slices of pie, you get candy in a flavor/color to match

- **Candyland—OBVIOUS!**

THE VIP TICKET
TO AN MVP SUMMER

MVP Summer Goal: Look at Katy's text as the bona fide start of the MVP Summer—yesterday was just a warm-up

MVP Summer Action: Introduce Diego to Katy Harris with zero awkward moments

Post-Day Analysis:
June 25

All of my dreams were bird related. They were fuzzy in my head (the dreams, not the birds—they had feathers) when I woke up, but I remembered one where a flock of birds carried Diego away. I think he was dreaming about birds, too, because I went to the bathroom at 3:33 in the morning, and he was doing birdcalls in his sleep.

Diego looked like the same person (except for the tan and the hair and the shell necklace and that he'd had to unzip his old Major League Baseball sleeping bag so his feet could hang out the end of it because he was so tall now). And he was the same,  right? Just because he had a new interest didn't mean he wasn't still Diego! After all, I had new things about myself since he'd been away, too.

But if I really was a good friend, I had to help Diego stay on his path, and his true love was sports and sports facts. Bird-watching could be a secondary interest, like me and poetry. This was Diego, who had once called the Topps baseball card company to suggest it improve its cards by including baseball history cards with black-and-white photos and old-timey players. He might have liked birdcalls, but they weren't his **CALLING**.

So, getting ready, I thought it would probably take only one Braves games for him to remember the true meaning of summer, and his true self. (There's nothing wrong with birdcalls, of course, but if you can choose between a base-ball play-by-play or a parrot's screeches, you'd be nuts to pick the parrot.) Then I'd tell his true self we were headed for an MVP Summer.

I got a text.

> **Katy:** Didn't u say u & Diego going 2 Braves game today? I'm singing the anthem!
>
> **Gabby:** What? NO WAY.
>
> **Katy:** There's a reception during game. Can get u in. By the press box!!
>
> **Gabby:** NO. WAY.

I wanted to type: "**SEE**? The **MVP SUMMER** is not putting too much pressure on things because you just invited me to the **COOLEST MVP SUMMER** kickoff event of **ALL TIME**!" But I was too grateful to point out her error.

The message came as Diego and I were trying to get the most blueberry-filled of my dad's blueberry pancakes on our plates. Diego was talking to my dad about a family of robins that my dad had been feeding stale tortillas to over the spring. Ugh.

But the press box! How could Diego not remember his beloved dream when he'd be right there in Dream Central?? And besides, he'd also meet Katy Harris. He would probably have an instant crush on her and probably want to point out key moments in the history of people singing the national anthem at ball games. I didn't think that would impress her necessarily, but it would be a solid reminder to Diego of how good he was at this sports stuff.

"Wow, cool," Diego said when I told him. It wasn't the all-caps **WOW! COOL!** I'd expected, but that would change when we arrived.

So, with a few more texts, we decided to meet Katy in the bottom of the fourth inning. And up until then, everything was going great.

First off, it was Bobblehead Day and even if you're someone like me who never necessarily thought they wanted a bobblehead, when someone gives you one for free **AND** it's a bobblehead of Homer the Brave, the most amazing mascot in baseball history, well, you suddenly love bobbleheads. Plus, there was almost no line for the hot pretzel the size of our faces. That's just plain good luck and who could argue with good luck?

Peter wasn't even being that annoying, because he'd

GOOD LUCK SIGNS

HOMER THE BRAVE BOBBLEHEAD

GIANT PRETZEL

brought along his friend Jared and they were busy talking about the Robofang movie they'd finally seen the other day. We settled into our seats and Diego took a deep breath of the ballfield air and said, "Smell that fresh mowed grass. It's good to be home."

He sounded like an old man who'd returned from a long trip at sea, but at least he was talking about baseball grass and not birds! Truthfully, the air smelled more like hot dogs and personal pizzas but I wasn't going to correct him, because it still smelled good. Like a ballpark.

"This is gonna be the best summer ever!" he said as we tore our pretzel in half. I was **THIS CLOSE** to saying, "Not just the best summer, but an MVP Summer!" but I waited. I needed an even bigger moment. Then we held up our pretzel pieces and were about to clink them together like we were doing a toast. (There would be no satisfying clinking noise, but it was fun anyway.) But Diego held up a hand signaling to pause. "Do you hear that? I could swear I hear a yellow-rumped warbler's call."

The crowd was so loud and chattering around us that the bird would have had to have been the size of a pro wrestler to be heard above all the noise but then, sure enough, on the railing a few rows down, a gray bird with a yellow butt landed.

THE YELLOW-RUMPED WARBLER BEING A BUTTHEAD....

"Oh my gosh, this is amazing," Diego said. "They usually don't like to leave the woods. He must be on a mission."

"Maybe he doesn't want to miss any of the game," I said, pointing to the field where the bird-free game was starting.

"That's a great sign, though," Diego said. "I can't wait for us to go bird-watching. You're gonna love it."

I swallowed my pretzel and smiled, but I wondered how I was going to help Diego come back to his senses. Unless you were lazy-rivering and randomly spied a bird flying overhead, bird-watching was not MVP Summer caliber.

"That's Katy," I said, grateful to change the subject. I pointed to her striding onto the field, wearing a red dress with silver sparkles on it and cute blue flats. Since the closest I've ever come to knowing a famous person was when my uncle Emilio was on the news because a tree fell in his front yard, it was super-duper **AMAZING** to see a person I knew walking to the middle of a Major League Baseball field and be given a microphone to sing the "Star-Spangled Banner" for **THE WHOLE STADIUM** (and everyone at home . . . !!).

And Katy wasn't just a person I knew; she was my friend.

"Whoa," Diego said under his breath. "I can't believe you know her." I felt relieved that he seemed to be developing a crush as he watched her hit the high notes. I had no proof of this crush, but it seemed like everyone in the stadium was in awe of Katy, so why not Diego, too? And if he had a crush, he'd have less time for birds. Plus, it meant some Diego things were still as I thought they'd be.

The game unfolded perfectly, with action and suspense

to keep Diego's focus on the field. The Braves started out the first inning by allowing no runners on base and by scoring two runs!

In the second, we watched a foul ball from one of the Cubs fly into the stands just a few rows below ours when Diego smacked his forehead. "I can't believe I never told you this! But did you know that Rawlings baseballs are made in Costa Rica?" A baseball fact! Thank goodness!

"I think I knew that. But the factory used to be Haiti," Louie pitched in. "Then the company got worried about political unrest."

Political unrest was definitely not something you'd think you'd hear at a ballpark. But it was a very Louie thing to say. And not bird-related.

"How do you know that?" my dad asked her.

"I stay informed." Louie shrugged. "I'm good to keep around."

"You are a keeper." They gave each other a kiss. Peter and his friend groaned.

"Ugh, doesn't anyone realize me and Jared are eight and don't want to witness those moments?"

"Well, you get to witness all of them by yourselves because me and Diego have to go to the exclusive, no-eight-year-olds-allowed reception now!"

Diego sprung up. "Woo-hoo! Let's go."

"Are you both sure you know how to get there? It's just down the concourse and then through the . . ." My dad looked nervous. It was the first time Diego and I were going to be allowed to walk around the park without an adult chaperone.

"Dad! We've been here what? Four hundred thousand times?" That was an exaggeration but we definitely had been there a lot.

"I know, I know. Just text me when you get there."

"It's only about six hundred feet away," I said. "But okay." Phone freedom was the **BEST**! Dad still looked worried, but he was willing to let me and Diego head off on our own because the phones gave him confidence he could locate us if he needed to.

"Your signal is good?" Louie asked.

"If she gets lost, can't we just leave her here?" Peter joked, and Jared laughed. Joke was on them, though, since the number-one best place to be left was probably a ballpark!

I was trying to figure out how to check my signal when I got a text from Katy, wondering where we were. "Yup, that's from inside the ballpark! Let's go, Diego."

Katy was outside the reception room like she said

she'd be. She was wearing a Braves warm-up jacket over the dress she'd sung the anthem in. Diego looked really impressed. "Do you know she has more than a million subscribers on YouTube? I looked her up earlier."

"Just don't be weird," I whispered to him. "She's really a normal person." I wasn't sure I believed this, but it sounded good.

"I know, but a normal person with outstanding data."

"Diego! Saying someone has outstanding data is super weird!"

"Okay, okay."

Katy saw us and waved. "Gabby girl! You're here!" She ran up and gave me a huge hug. Then she turned to Diego . . . and got super quiet. She looked at her shoes and then at me and then, finally, at Diego.

"I'm Diego," he said first. "Your performance was awesome!" I thought Diego would be kind of nervous to meet Katy but if anything, **SHE** seemed nervous. Or maybe she'd changed her mind about inviting us both along?

"Thanks. I, um, like your necklace," she said.

"Thanks, it was a gift. Oh, and I saw your talent show performance. Your stage show rules. There was this Swiss Hornussen player who quit the sport to become a pop star. His awesome light show made him famous in Switzerland. But your dancers are even better than his lasers."

Oh my gosh. Had Diego really brought up a random Hornussen fact? That was almost as bad as birds. (**OLD FUTURE ME**, because you'll have no reason to remember Hornussen, it is a strange Swiss sport with like a thousand odd rules that Diego loves a ridiculous amount.)

"Oh, thank you." Katy still seemed . . . not like Katy. This was awful. She must have thought Diego was a total weirdo.

Diego at that point launched into a whole history of the game. My stomach lurched. What if Katy thought he was unbearable? What if he thought Katy was a snob?

"A Nouss whizzing by a striker and they never saw it again!" I heard Diego say, knowing it was the end of his favorite Hornussen story. This was when Katy would wonder why she even invited me here.

... A NOUSS WHIZZING BY A STRIKER AND THEY NEVER SAW IT AGAIN!

But she laughed a little, like she knew what Hornussen was. "Sounds fun," she said. "Should we go inside? There's food." I started to think maybe Katy didn't know how excited I was to be there.

"I'm starving," I said, even though I wasn't that hungry. I just wanted to say something. "Thanks so much for inviting us."

Katy shrugged like it was no big deal, then turned to head in. "I saw mini cheeseburgers in there."

"Why is food so much better in mini sizes?" I asked, trying to get the conversation to feel fun.

"Because the only foods that come in mini sizes are always foods people like to begin with," Diego said.

"Mini food is our birthday party food of choice!" I reminded Diego. How perfectly had I worked that in?

"Oh, yeah," he said, then told Katy, "Gabby and I were born a day apart. Hopefully you'll be at our party."

Katy actually blushed and said, still in a soft voice, "I would love that."

"We have to plan that," I reminded Diego.

"Yep, but we have time." Ugh, when had Diego become so easygoing about plans? When would he say, "What's the plan?"

But Katy was leading us to a hallway where there were doors to the skyboxes that looked out over the field. The reception for Katy and several other special guests (a group of Atlanta fourth graders who'd gone to the White House for winning the state science fair) was being held in one that was supersized and right alongside the press box. You could actually see into the press box, where journalists and radio commentators watched and called the game. I thought Diego's lower face was going to fall off, his jaw dropped so far.

Diego stopped to look at a wall full of team memorabilia—old uniforms and gloves worn by Braves greats, old scorecards, newspaper clippings—and Katy came up and tapped my shoulder. Was she mad I'd brought Diego?

"This is so great, Katy," I said. "But is everything okay?"

"You didn't tell me Diego is so **COOL**," she said. "And cute."

WHAT? Diego? Cool? And cute?

"That Diego?" I pointed at him, looking very Regular Old Diego with his nose almost pressed against a glass case of Braves souvenirs. There was a smear of mustard on

CUTE AND COOL ???

his cheek. "You're way cooler than Diego."

I felt a little bad saying it, because Diego was my friend, but really, Katy had no reason to be nervous around him. I'd known Diego my whole life. He'd had crushes on people but no one that I knew had ever had a crush on him. And Katy was like a Baby Beyoncé. Baby Beyoncés didn't have to be shy!

"Yeah," she said, glancing at him. Diego grinned widely and started walking back toward us. "Don't say anything to him!"

I wouldn't, because who knew what I would say? I was kind of shocked. Diego was still my friend Diego, but there were so many new layers to him I wasn't used to. Still, it was time to enjoy my surroundings. MVP Summer Me knew that was a good thing to do. The skybox had a great view of the field. The one thing I didn't love was the glass wall between us and the crowd. Part of what's awesome about baseball games is sitting in my folding seat with the rest of the fans, right out in the open air. But the skybox was humming with excitement, just in a different way. Plus, as I smelled the food, my stomach rumbled.

"So you were in Costa Rica?" Katy said to Diego as we headed toward the buffet. She seemed like she maybe had pulled herself together. "I've always wanted to go there."

"You should go," he said. "Especially if you like birds."

Oh. **NO.**

I put five mini cheeseburgers on my plate and started to eat them too fast as I tried to decide what would be worse: Katy being all crushy and weird over Diego or Diego boring Katy to death with the birds. "Or wildlife of any kind, really. Or the environment. Or coffee. They have good coffee."

Katy giggled. "I like most of those things. Not coffee."

I knew it was fine if my friend liked my other friend, I did. But everything was happening so fast I couldn't process it. If only we lived in a bubble where I could help Diego re-assimilate slowly. Or somewhere where I could

FLIRTING
FRIENDS ?

EAT A
CHEESEBURGER

NEW-assimilate to **NEW** Diego.

Diego and Katy kept chatting while I sort of stood there shoving mini cheeseburgers into my mouth, thinking how one of the reasons I liked baseball was that the rules mostly stayed the same. I snapped a photo of the skybox view and sent it to Johnny with a smiley face. Then I semi-regretted it because what if he felt bad I hadn't invited him? I hadn't totally told him about Diego because people didn't always get that we really were **JUST FRIENDS**. I planned to have them meet this summer and everything would be very clear. Still, I waited and waited for his response. I checked the time. It had been almost a **MINUTE**! Oh no, I'd blown everything.

DING! A smiley—no wink—from Johnny! Plus a baseball mitt and a sunshine emoji! That was good, right?

I was debating the right emoji response, but then Damien Trost walked into the reception room. Damien **TROST**, one of the **BEST** relief pitchers in Braves history. My dad had once taken me to an event where he was going to be signing baseballs but it had been so crowded that when he signed mine, the people in charge had to move us along before I could say that he was one of my favorite pitchers.

"What is Damien Trost doing here?" I said, after gulping

down the mini burger I should have chewed better.

"He's doing a meet and greet," Katy said. "I forgot to tell you. My mom and aunt have been waiting all morning for this." She pointed at two women who were lined up alongside some ropes I hadn't noticed that led to an area with a photo backdrop where Damien Trost was talking to waiting fans.

THE AMAZING DAMIEN TROST

Katy's mom and aunt looked like taller, older versions of her. They also looked really excited. Louie once made my dad jealous talking about how handsome Damien Trost was. I didn't know about that; I just knew he had the best curve balls I'd ever seen. If I shook his hand, would his magic pitching powers rub off on me??? If that happened, I could go **PRO** tomorrow! I would definitely not have to play catcher! My hand started to tingle waiting for its new pitching abilities.

"Damien Trost is, like, Gabby's favorite pitcher," Diego said. "After Sandy Koufax, of course." He said it with so much best-friend authority that I felt bad about not being more enthusiastic about his newfound love of birds.

We got into line together. Now that I knew Katy was crushing on Diego, I felt incredibly strange. I'd really thought it would be the other way around, with Diego tongue-tied by her, but here he was, saying something about a game we'd seen where Damien had not only gotten a save for the game but had also hit a walk-off home run. Katy was smiling and nodding at the story, saying she remembered that game, and I felt a little sick to my stomach and didn't know if it was nervousness to be so close to my hero, or the many mini cheeseburgers mingling with pretzels and blueberry pancakes, or wondering if it was even possible to re-assimilate Diego when he seemed like a **WHOLE NEW PERSON**!

Then Damien Trost looked over at us and started to walk right toward us! Was it possible he'd seen the story in the Atlanta paper about the regional game? But I hadn't even pitched that much! Maybe he could tell that I'd been forced to play catcher and was coming over to tell me he was going to fix everything.

But he wasn't coming over to talk to me. And not even

to Katy, though he did say, "Excellent job on the anthem," to her. No, he went right to Diego and pointed at his **SHELL NECKLACE**!

"Did you buy that in Playa Conchal?" Damien said to him. Diego touched the necklace and said, "Actually, one of my dad's lab partners' kids made it for me as a gift, because I helped tutor her in science. But her mom runs a restaurant near Playa Conchal."

He hadn't mentioned that to me. Costa Rica Diego had a whole life that Peach Tree Diego hadn't told me about. He named the restaurant and Damien Trost got really excited about a plantain cake they made. And then Diego was talking to Damien Trost like they were old buddies!

"So you lived there? Amazing. Did you see the sea turtles at Tortuguero?"

"Yeah, but the sloths were my favorite," Diego said. "Gabby, remember the one I told you about?" Diego gestured for me to come join the conversation.

"The one who was fast, for a sloth?" I remembered Diego had mentioned the sloth right around when I was starting Piper Bell and I'd been a little jealous that his life seemed way simpler than mine at the time.

"I didn't know Costa Rica had sloths," Katy said. Sloth talk had her at ease. "They're my favorite animal."

"I would have loved to see that," Damien said. I was about to say something funny about sloths—I didn't know what, but I just wanted a chance to talk to my favorite pitcher ever—but then he shook all our hands and said he had to get back to the meet and greet.

But even though Damien Trost, all-star reliever, was in our midst, the whole skybox seemed focused on Diego, wondering how he knew a Major League pitcher. Even though if anything, Damien Trost seemed more interested in Diego's Costa Rica–ness than Diego was in Damien Trost's Major League–ness. What if Diego just wished he could go back? What if he never asked what the plan was? Or worse, **DIDN'T CARE**?

I knew what I had to do: I'd have to make MVP Summer even more awesome.

MVP Summer Points: 50 points out of 100 for a good start (50 lost for mini-burger-muddled-feeling stomach issues)

MVP Summer Tally: 460

THINK SMALL

When hunger strikes
You know what's nice?
You might be surprised
It's not an X-large cheese pizza
Or anything oversized

The best things for the growling
Aren't what you think
Not a dozen donuts or a whole cake
Nope, the perfect food to fill you
Is as small as you can make

Tiny burgers that fit in your palm
Mini corn dogs on a stick
Baby burritos or a pie made small
Nibble-sized foods are great
Because you can eat each and all

So, next time your tummy rumbles
Don't look for something big
Instead change your mind about what's a feast
And I think you'll soon find
That size matters the least.

FOR THE BIRDS

MVP Summer Goal: Ensure Diego's birding outing doesn't make him a social outcast and be there with an awesome alternative when his new hobby flies the coop

MVP Summer Strategy: A sacrifice bunt, only in this case I'd be giving up my Saturday morning

Post-Day Analysis:
June 26

So, maybe I'd been overreacting to New Diego too much. Okay, he really liked birds and wouldn't take off his con-versation-piece necklace. Damien Trost had one just like it and the bird thing would probably die out. (Diego's obses-sion, not the bird populace, which I wish well and hope goes on tweeting and flying until forever!)

Diego was clearly just in post-vacation mode. I'd worn my Mickey ears for several weeks after my first trip to Disney World and truly believed adults should drive more like Mr. Toad. I'd been seven years old at the time, but still.

Diego had liked things in the past that I hadn't understood. Like the Boston Red Sox, for half a season, and, one Olympics, curling. (He thought it was really fascinating. I disagreed.) But those had been passing things and he'd gotten over them.

If I was really an MVP and his supportive friend, I could at least try to play along with birding. Especially because I really thought yesterday's Diego Fan Club was sort of a fluke. I believed Katy had a crush and even that Damien Trost had liked Diego's Costa Rican accessories, but that was all like a magic spell. I knew Diego well enough to know that his luck wouldn't last forever. That wasn't a mean thing, just a fact. Like, anytime we went roller skating, the second Diego realized he'd done two loops without falling, he'd immediately crash into a wall.

So this morning, I'd agreed to a "birding" expedition. Partly because Diego had texted me to say, *Will you be joining us on the birding expedition?*

And I thought, *Who's us?* Then I imagined Diego out in the woods or whatever with his binoculars and his bird guide and some kind of strange bird hat waiting for whoever "us" was and no one showing up. Or people showing up by accident thinking birding was code for a dance flash mob or something and they'd arrive and be disappointed when Diego tried to get them excited over a red-bellied gobble-wobbler (not a real bird, though it probably could be).

Diego's mom swung by to pick me up and I noticed the whole way to the expedition site, he was checking things on his phone. Which I thought was a little rude but he showed me that he was doing a peek at weather conditions and getting very excited about the species we'd be able to see.

"Well, maybe we'll be able to see them," he said. "Birds are like good base runners, Gabby. Just when you think you know what they're up to, they pull a fast one."

It felt like

a desperate grab to make birding appeal to me but I didn't let on. "I can't wait to see it happen. Or **NOT** see it!"

"It would be awesome to see a western kingbird this summer," he said. He showed me a photo on his phone of a kind of mean-looking bird with a gray stripe across its eyes and a fly in its beak. Its belly was yellowish-orange. "There's only been one sighted in Georgia in the last several years but they fly in from Texas sometimes."

"We'll keep an eye out," I said in my best excited voice. It was a good thing I was going with him, I thought, because he was never going to see that bird and then he'd feel extra let down by the lack of birding interest in Peach Tree. He'd need me around. Maybe birding was fine for the jungle but we had so many other things to do here. I'd cheer him up after with a round of mini golf. Then I'd fill him on the excellent MVP Summer I had planned over an ice cream flavor we had never tried. Even if it wasn't

BLUISH GRAY →

LOOKS MEAN!!!

YELLOW

GRAY

THE WESTERN KINGBIRD

the huge moment I thought the announcement needed, it would make Diego feel better.

But when his mom pulled the van up, there was a crowd. Like a good-sized crowd of kids our age, waiting outside this small wooden building that had once been a schoolhouse and now was full of signs and exhibits about the various wildlife in the surrounding preserve. Maybe people really **HAD** thought there would be a flash mob. Unfortunately, I'm not much of a dancer and neither is Diego.

"It looks like a few people didn't make it," Diego said.

What? I thought. But I said, "How'd you get such a big crowd?"

"My pictures," Diego said. "You know how I had that BirdBios Instagram of all my Costa Rican bird friends?"

"Oh, yeah," I said. Diego had sent me the link but I'd only gone online to look once. Trying to be sneaky, I tapped open the app on my phone and, sure enough, DiegosBird-Bios had about one thousand followers. Jeez. I followed it, because it was the Good Friend thing to do.

"One great thing about being back is I can post much more frequently," Diego said. "My followers are really interested in my pics."

Oh-kaaaaay. Maybe Diego was more devoted to the

bird thing than I thought. But it was still good I was there to help him because looking at photos of birds with funny captions is a lot different than standing in the woods, watching for them. I was going to help keep things lively and fun! (So no one died of boredom.)

When we hopped out of the car and Diego greeted his adoring fans, I came face-to-face with Johnny. Who looked, as usual, **REALLY CUTE**. I looked like a total dork with my binoculars and a satchel of supplies and my other birding gear. I also felt super nervous because I had finally settled on a reply to him of the final Braves game score and a series of three happy faces but all he'd sent back was a thumbs-up. But was it a thumbs-up like "good for you" or a thumbs-up like "I hope to hold your hand again sometime!"?

"You like birding?" he exclaimed, and he **LOOKED** happy to see me. "You didn't

BIRDING HAT

BINOCULARS

BIRDING BOOKS

MILLION-POCKET BIRDING VEST

LUMPY SATCHEL

mention it. That's so cool." I noticed he had a bird guide-book in his hand and I wondered when everyone had decided to find birds so fascinating. I thought for a second I could take on birding the way I took on poetry but the truth was, I just didn't feel that way about birds. Poetry had sort of challenged me and even though I was mostly pretending to be a poet at first, I liked it. I was here for Diego today but I didn't think I would ever be a birder like he was. Or like Johnny seemed to be.

"Uh," I said. "I like birds. Mostly." (Mostly, I liked that they provided a little chirping during baseball games, or on sunny days. But the most attention I'd ever really paid to a bird was a pigeon that had followed me around the Target parking lot once, just staring at my hot dog from the café. Was there something wrong with me that this was not my idea of a great time?)

"I should have asked if you knew Diego," Johnny said. "I guess when I started reading his bird site, I thought he was like some kind of lone jungle superhero and no one really **KNEW** him, you know?"

Johnny's eyes got more sparkly than ever as he said this and it was hard not to be proud that he admired my best friend. I hoped that it wouldn't make him jealous when I said, "Diego is my best friend. From Luther."

"Of course you know all the cool people," Johnny said and smiled at me.

The cotton-candy feeling took over bigger than ever because Johnny seemed to definitely like me. But what would he think a few minutes into this birding borefest? I'd be consoling Diego when everyone bailed **AND** I'd probably have a broken heart, too.

"I do know a lot of cool people," I said to Johnny, hoping he'd get my very obvious hint that he was one of them.

Before Johnny could react to my sly compliment, Diego clapped his hands together and said, "Let's head into the woods, bird lovers!"

So we traipsed into the woods with Diego leading the way. I took a deep breath, expecting the happy walks to become dragging steps soon. Fortunately for Diego, I'd come prepared. I had snacks and a plan to keep things lively.

For a group of middle schoolers, we were tremendously quiet. No one was chatting and the silence felt really uncomfortable. It was the un-sound of Diego's social-life crisis looming. I pulled some Cheez-Its and juice boxes out of my bag. "Hey, I have snacks," I said, ripping open one of the bags. "Who wants some?" I crunched into a cracker.

All the bird watchers were now looking at me. Except Diego, who was a few steps ahead.

"You're going to scare the birds!" said one girl, spinning around with a furious look on her face. I had no idea birders could be so aggressive.

"Shh, everyone, this is exciting," Diego said, not even realizing his group was being incredibly rude to me, the snack bringer. He pointed to a far-off tree and put his binoculars to his eyes. "Do you all see it? A brown thrasher. Our state bird, so not an uncommon sighting, but a good omen for our day! Let's approach."

And everyone did as they were told, taking tiny quiet steps toward the boring brown bird. I checked on Johnny out of the corner of my eye and he had an interested expression on his face. I thought it was really polite and nice for him to be humoring Diego like that.

The bird was just sitting there in a tree. Doing nothing except moving its head in that twitchy bird way. A few of the people standing near me were getting bored, I could tell. I took out my phone. "If you like birds, have you seen this penguin video that's going around?" I swiped to a video I'd saved and showed my phone to a few of the birders. All I got in return were dirty looks.

"Oh yeah, I saw that," Johnny said appreciatively. At

least someone knew that the best birds were ones who could be adorable and entertaining. "But we should listen to Diego. I've never met anyone who knew so much about birds."

"Oh, look who just landed! That little guy seems calm and like a loner but he's actually very social," Diego said in a whisper, pointing at a new bird. "Eastern bluebirds really like to stick together, so if he's alone, he's probably looking for food."

I wanted to say, isn't that what birds of a feather do? *Stick together.* This was not new information even to a non-bird person, but Diego was acting like the host of some nature special.

Then Diego trailed off and gasped. "Hold on, everyone. It's a big moment here in the Little Blue Schoolhouse preserve. Listen to that." The bluebird sang out. A few seconds later, Diego did a call that was exactly like the bird's song.

Everyone got quiet. This was when they'd turn on Diego. My poor friend.

But then the bird sang back. The girl who'd yelled at me for the Cheez-Its applauded. "Ohmigosh, I'm sorry," she said as a few people turned to look at her. "That was just so exciting."

"It's okay to be excited," Diego said. And then the expedition turned into everyone asking Diego a million questions about the birds of Costa Rica and what it was like there and blah blah blah. I thought they would carry him on their shoulders all the way home.

HMMM...

Diego told some funny stories and then pointed at Johnny. "And let's thank Johnny for spreading the bird word around Peach Tree."

"Really?" I looked from Johnny to Diego. "So you guys have talked before, too?"

"We traded some messages about getting a bird group going here," Johnny said. "And then I found out Diego was also going to be a *Peach Tree Gazette* junior reporter, like me."

"Wait, you're doing that, too? You didn't say so!" I'd said that so loud that several birds flew from the trees they were hanging out in and the whole bird group shushed me at once.

But they didn't understand how loud my brain was. Diego and Johnny had become friends? Neither of them had told me about the other one before. It seemed like they'd jumped right over the part where I got to introduce them. And it seemed like they really liked each other, and would be hanging out all summer at the paper. I felt . . . jealous. That was **NOT** part of the plan.

"We didn't really have a chance to talk that much at Pizzabird," Johnny said. Quietly.

"Johnny and I went on a date, to see Pizzabird." I blurted it out, in a way that sounded like Johnny was something Diego and I were fighting over. But at least I whispered. Though people still turned around. They probably thought they were going to see a Pizzabird. As if Pizzabird had time for this.

Diego might have been a little surprised, but he seemed happy with the news and said, "Cool, I heard Pizzabird is good."

Wait, how could Diego not care that I was dating or that I'd seen Pizzabird without him?!

Maybe because my best friend was suddenly larger than life. Pizzabird himself wouldn't have gotten so much attention. And worse, I had been all wrong about his whole bird obsession being for the birds.

I had to go along with this for today at least. So I tried to stand politely while Diego demonstrated more bird-calls and everyone tried to copy them. I think he started his speech about how birds were like athletes but I was having trouble paying attention. We should have been sky-diving. Or at least bike riding at high speeds. My stomach growled. I snuck my packet of Cheez-Its from my bag and fished one out. I was about to covertly crunch it when a dark-bluish bird swooped down from the sky and plucked it right from my fingers!

I looked up and pointed at the culprit: "That bird stole my cracker!"

"A purple martin, and it's so shiny," Diego said as he watched the bird flutter overhead with my cracker in its mouth. "They're one of the most agile flyers!"

Everyone looked up at the bird, which seemed to be

taunting me with its antics, flying in a circle right over my head. I was almost enjoying the comedy until a wet splot of something hit my ear. The bird had **POOPED** on me! In front of everyone. Including Johnny. Who very nicely asked if I was okay but probably was also thinking how glad he was he hadn't been holding my hand.

That was kind of the moment I knew for sure birding wasn't for me. It was definitely not the beginning of MVP Summer.

So now, I'm writing this in my room, freshly showered, but still feeling sort of pooped-on. Not that Diego did anything wrong, but I thought I was there to help him and he didn't even need me.

"That's great," Dad had said when I told him about the crowd that had come to Diego's birding event, not mentioning that I had not loved it. "Kids today are so much more accepting of each other's unique interests. When I was your age, try and get someone to talk about Shakespeare with me and—nothing. Or sometimes worse than nothing."

But I wasn't accepting of Diego's unique interests! **OR** at least not that he was more interested in them than **ANY-THING ELSE**. And his unique interests had pooped on me, so the feeling was mutual!

Sure, birding was fine for someone else. But Diego and I

had always been about sports and summer fun and I had it **ALL PLANNED OUT**! Now he was totally occupied with a bird club and he had a job at the paper with Johnny and all I had was **ZERO INTEREST** in birds and a place on a team where I was forced to play catcher.

How could I make this an MVP Summer if the game had totally changed?

MVP Summer Points: A big fat goose egg. AKA zero. Actually MINUS 20 points, for the poop.

MVP Summer Tally: 440, plus an overwhelming new fear of birds flying overhead

PITCH PERFECT

MVP Summer Goal: To sweat my butt off in catcher's gear because I'm part of a team (also, to win the game because I could really use it right now).

MVP Summer Strategy: ~~Have a good attitude, try hard, etc.~~ Not play catcher at all!

Post-Day Analysis:
June 28

Since birding, everything felt topsy-turvy. The bright spot was that last night after birding, Diego had spied the Freezemobile ice cream truck at the park where we'd have our birthday party and texted me. We both tried a new ice cream bar that was green and supposedly tropical but tasted like what would happen if a lime threw up. But at least it was an MVP Summer activity. Not the big one I needed to kick off the whole thing. And Diego still recapped the whole bird event. Then he had his cousin's graduation party to go to and I had baseball practice and Katy was rehearsing and Johnny was at something called Calculus Camp.

How could the MVP Summer really happen if no one had time to even hear the **PLAN**???

When I arrived at our first all-star game today, I was in a funk. I didn't even want to play because the couple practices we had had so far had been awful. I really didn't love playing catcher. I mostly hated it. The gear was sweaty and all the crouching and having to look directly at the position I *did* want to play . . .

CATCHING VS. PITCHING

CATCHING

- Too much equipment—welcome to SweatyTown

- Crouching gets very uncomfortable, plus . . .

- Butt-level with every batter (see: crouching)

- Pitchers sometimes wave off your signs and throw whatever they want

- (Reason above even worse if you have pitching expertise that is being **IGNORED**)

PITCHING

- Central to the action and standing on highest point of the field

- Winding up to throw is one of the most beautiful motions you can make

- Eye-to-eye with the batter—**DRAMA**!

- Freedom to wave off catcher's signs if you have a better idea

- When you're a pitcher, you just know: You should **PITCH**!

Still, I wanted to win some games, even if there wasn't for sure a trophy or anything. Being an all-star meant being adaptable was part of the job. It wasn't as though Coach Hollylighter was treating me unfairly: everyone had a new position to play and no one was necessarily happy about it.

Devon, for example, whose glinty-eyed stare was intimidating on even her happiest days, was full-on glinty-eyed **GLARING** at the empty shortstop position as she grumbled clearly angry noises that could only be translated by other disappointed people. Like Mario, who kicked the dirt hard enough to create a large dust cloud and said "third base" like it was a word we shouldn't be allowed to use.

By demonstrating my supreme adaptability, I was way ahead of Devon and Mario. Not that being Zen about things is a contest but, fine, I was enjoying it.

Being adaptable got easier when I got to the field and learned that Casey was too nervous to pitch and Alfonso was on vacation. "Are you sure, Casey?" Coach asked him. "You looked good in practice." (He really hadn't.)

To answer, Casey excused himself to go to the bathroom. Definitely a case of the yips, plus maybe something else.

So . . . Coach Hollylighter said that Devon or I would have to pitch and we'd flip for it. At that same moment, I spied **JOHNNY** show up. I'd only **CASUALLY** invited him over text with a lot of "if u feel like it, we have a game" kind of lines and here he was—**EARLY**—and, like he'd texted, he'd come with his sister. Sasha looked like a Sasha. She was glamorous with big sunglasses and a black dress and I was glad he'd told me she was his sister or I would have worried about how frizzy my ponytail was.

For a split second I thought about saying that I'd talk to Casey to help him with his case of nerves. I knew what those were like. But I *really* wanted to pitch. And with Johnny here, I felt more than ever like I **NEEDED** to pitch. I wanted him to be able to point to me on the mound, at the center of it all, and say, "That's Gabby," and get an admiring look in his eye.

Plus, I could see from the extra bit of glint in Devon's eye that she wanted to bail on shortstop as much as I wanted to not be catching. So why did I have to take the high road?

"Coach Daniels, will you do the honors?" Coach Hollylighter asked, handing him the quarter. She was watching the other team take batting practice and I thought at least a teensy part of her should be glad Devon or I would be pitching since the other team looked good. I wasn't nervous though, just prepared. I needed three things to happen in order to make this an MVP Summer–worthy day:

Win the coin toss.

Pitch a great game.

Allow Coach Hollylighter to see how wrong she'd been to switch our positions for the summer.

If I pitched well enough to win the game, **EVERYONE** could have their old positions back. That was my theory, anyway. Then the entire team would know that I hadn't just been playing for myself but for all of them.

Coach Daniels put Devon and me on either side of him, so we were facing off. It didn't matter that Devon was my friend in that moment because any time you were standing face-to-face with Devon with something hanging in the balance, it was an instant showdown.

"Devon, call it," Coach Daniels said as he flicked the shiny coin up in the air. I swear that Devon's glinty-eyed glare was able to see the coin's sides as it turned, and when she shouted "Heads!" I thought for sure she'd perfectly clocked it.

Coach Daniels plucked the coin from the air and slapped it on his hand. "Tails! Gabby, you pitch!"

Devon frowned and looked down at his hand as if she didn't believe him, scowling when it was the tails side facing up. But then she shot me a grin and said, "Make them come to their senses." So she'd been thinking the same way as me. She wiped her grin away and added, "I mean it." Terrifying.

FAILURE
IS
NOT
AN
OPTION.

The game was about to start. My parents and Peter were in the stands, and Diego was coming to cover the game for the *Gazette*. Johnny and Sasha were looking in my direction and Johnny waved. I waved back in what I hoped was a fashionable way but that might have looked like I was trying to shoo a fly. If I pitched well, not only would Johnny's sister encourage him to ask me on more dates and hold my hand A **LOT**, but Diego would cover the game in glowing terms that would work a spell on Coach Hollylighter! Bonus: Diego might also have been transported to a time before birds. He'd remember the true meaning of summer. Baseball was magic like that.

Or at least I was hoping it would be today.

The problem was, the game started out kind of a dozer. A snooze. A yawn. I'm not saying it was boring to **ME**, because it wasn't. Baseball is a game that takes patience to appreciate.

And I appreciated it. It was a total pitcher's game. As in, the Jefferson team's pitcher, Alexander something, was a perfect match for me and by the third inning the score was 0–0. (This sounds dull but when pitchers are matched well and keeping their batters off base, it's like a very exciting **DUEL**! P.S. I know nothing about real duels, and they sound **REALLY SCARY**, but our innings had that back-and-forth, what-will-they-do-next feeling to them. Which is what I imagine a duel is like. Except way scarier.)

So Alexander and I were knocking it out of the park. (Except no one was knocking it out of the park. Because we were that good.)

The batters coming up against us could only manage pop flies, or little grounders that barely went out of the infield, at best. Easy outs.

Sadly, even though a smart fan—like Diego—knew this was a good game, I felt like the fans didn't agree. It was a hot

PERFECT MATCH PITCHERS

ALEXANDER

M

Georgia day when the air moved not at all. The crowd wanted big action. Johnny was watching intently but his sister was fanning herself with her hat. Even Diego looked a little blah as he made notes on a steno pad.

Here are a few of the more-or-less non-happenings that can make a baseball game feel a little, say, **MEH**. (**OLD ME**, in case baseball has changed one hundred years in the future—because some people want it to and I won't even get into that—this will remind you of some of the things casual fans don't like about baseball games at times.)

Middling hits—Pop fly balls that make it just into the outfield and are easy outs, or little grounders that fielders can quickly scoop up and toss to the base. The audience likes bigger hits: fast-moving line drives and long-distance fly balls that look like they could be home runs.

Players left on base—This is fine with me as a pitcher, because if I let one person on base, I'd rather no one else gets a hit to move that base runner. But if inning after inning a batter gets on base and then nothing else happens, the people watching get frustrated.

No throws from the corner or "two on, two outs" situations—A throw from the corner is when a third baseman has to get the ball all the way to first to make an out, or the opposite. It's a big exciting moment. And a "two on, two outs" situation means that the batting team has two runners on base and two outs, which is a boost for suspense.

Fans who are just there—This is my top-secret playbook and these insights will never leave these pages so I can be totally honest. The people who say baseball is boring . . . well, they are a huge part of the problem. My theory is, people today are so used to **THINGS! HAPPENING! ALL! THE! TIME!!!**—in sports, in the news, on the internet (the cute puppy video you missed today that no one cares about tomorrow)—they don't have a lot of patience to stay into a game where sometimes things are more thoughtful. Baseball is very **ZEN**. I think, personally, if you breathe deeply and focus on the field, it's relaxing until it's exciting again. But not everyone sees it that way.

WAY MORE EXCITING THAN IT LOOKS!

It always seems to me that the games fans want to see have lots of scoring and big plays or at least a lot of near-scoring and suspense.

But you don't really need anything to be **HUGE** for baseball to be interesting: even when it's quiet, **SO MUCH IS HAPPENING**! The pitcher is thinking about her next pitch but also the ball she *just* pitched. The infield is eyeballing the baserunners. The baserunners are watching the batter and looking for openings to steal a base. The outfield has their eye on the batter and their bodies ready to sprint toward a fly ball. The batter is considering whether to bunt or swing big while also keeping an eye on the ball and knowing **NOT** to swing if the pitch is too high, or outside, or something else not worth trying to hit. The catcher is watching the field but also the batter and sending signals to the pitcher about what to throw.

UGH. If people don't understand how exciting that is, there's something wrong with them. (My dad says I am like a peppy preteen optimist with the heart of an elderly curmudgeon, which is like a crusty old man who can be very stubborn about certain things. **BUT I SHOULD BE STUBBORN** about this. Besides, I'm not a curmudgeon. I'm a connoisseur.)

But today the non-connoisseurs in
the stands were fidgeting or checking their phones (darn phones) or
in the case of my brother, Peter,
very clearly playing dead
by slumping dramatically
over his seat. Johnny did
seem to be watching but
then I saw Sasha tap his
shoulder and say something.
Then she went and stood in
the shade! If this didn't get more
exciting, he'd leave!

PETER
PLAYING
DEAD
"☠"

Also, it was possibly too quiet, rather than the quiet
where there's a hum of something about to happen. How
would I remind Diego how exciting it was to be here,
on the ballfield, rather than birding, when right now felt
JUST LIKE birding? (Actually, it felt like we were watching dead birds.) How would I get Sasha to tell Johnny I
was the coolest girl he could ever meet?

I was up to bat. I could change everything. I took a
few practice swings—big, juicy swings so that every fan
on the bleachers would have to watch. Then I wiped the
sweat from my brow and tapped my bat against home plate

a few times. I had to look like a star for Johnny and his sister, plus I had to give Diego the story of a lifetime and remind him how awesome baseball and summer could be. It was a lot to do in one at bat.

Then a bird landed on the chain-link above me. It was probably called the Diego Attention-Stealing Tweetmonster. I stuck my tongue out at it.

Alexander wound up. I knew it would be a fastball. I sucked air through my teeth and swung, hard, but only got the tippy-tip of my bat to touch the ball. Still, it was a hit, just to the left of Alexander, who couldn't quite reach it. **YES!**

I HUSTLED.

But not for long enough. Midway to first base, I did what you never do.

I **LOOKED**. Looked over, to see if Diego was getting this, to see if Sasha looked impressed, to see if Johnny was holding up a sign that said he was totally in like with me.

I snapped back to my run for first before I could see any of those things but it was too late. I hurled myself at the base as the ball came flying into the baseman's mitt . . . and propelled myself **RIGHT OVER** the base. I was out.

It was the bird-pooping-on-my-head moment I hadn't seen coming.

I knew I had to brush it off, but I had to admit, I wished for a second I could just hide in the catcher's gear so no one could see my face for a while.

Finally, in the bottom of the seventh, Mario grabbed a big ol' hunk of one of Alexander's fastballs and hit a solo home run! The crowd went berserk! Of course, it was because they thought a home run was more exciting than the inner workings of the pitcher's brain. But hey, if anyone is going to put points on the board, of course I want it to be **MY TEAM**. We were up 1–0 in the bottom of the seventh.

That meant I only needed to pitch two more good innings and we could totally win this game. I was feeling very upbeat again when Mario rounded home. I was on deck to bat and yelled to the dugout, "Show Mario the love!"

Diego overheard from his lawn chair behind the backstop because he said, as I took my practice swings, "Hey, wait, you and Mario get along now?" The question came out of left field. Well, not really, since before Diego had left he'd known Mario as my prime nemesis.

"Yeah, it's a Piper Bell alliance," I said, hoping that *alliance* made it feel more like a good-teammates thing than a super-close-friend thing. But then I felt bad for saying it that way and said, "Actually, Mario is pretty nice if you're on his team. We just butted heads as competitors."

"Oh, okay," Diego replied, like this was a known fact and I didn't used to get really worked up about games against Mario before. "That's good, then." I guess I thought he'd **CARE** more that I was friends with awful, evil Mario (who really wasn't those things). Why was I so bothered by Diego's changes and he didn't seem to be nervous about any of mine?

We didn't score any other runs that inning—our batters after Mario struck out—and I was back on the mound in the top of the eighth and the sky clouded over, really fast. Georgia in summer is like that, and, I swear, it had decided to be like that during the game just to mess with me. At least it was a hot day, so when the first few little drops fell, no one went running, because it probably felt refreshing.

Still, when I tossed out my first pitch to the batter at the plate, I could feel something was off. The ball was a perfect "Come on and hit me!" pitch right in the strike zone. The batter swung and nailed a sweet grounder to center field. He got on base.

I took a deep breath and told myself it could have been much worse. It also could have been much better if I hadn't been forced to practice at catcher the last few days. But I cleared my head and struck the next batter out. I stood tall on my mound and checked the bases around me. I squeezed my glove in and out three times to get my head straight. And, okay, I glanced over at Johnny and his sister, but they were gone. Where'd they go? They were missing this. My heart sank. What if they'd left because of my base-running flub?

But, pitching. I was pitching, not catching. I had to do it right. Jefferson's big hitter came up to the plate. If she got a home run off me, they'd be up 2–1 and I'd just have to work that much harder in the next inning. **OR**, if it started raining harder, the umps would call the game and might hand the win to Jefferson.

And of course, the big hitter . . . sent the ball straight up in the air, just as the rain started to pour faster. I jogged forward, squinting to see the ball, and there it was! It came down, perfect, into my glove.

The base runner on first, hoping the rain would slow me down, must have thought he could make a quick move to second, though. He started to run after the ball was in my glove and I turned and hurled the ball to Devon with perfect precision. She caught it like her life depended on it and tagged the base seconds before the runner made it!

Just like that, we had all our outs. And the rain stopped!

A baseball miracle!

Plus, how could Diego not have excellent material for his write-up? There was drama, there was action, there was *extreme weather*! Then sunshine.

The whole thing was a sportswriter's dream, if you asked me.

OTHER SPORTSWRITER'S DREAMS

- A basketball team that is down all game finally closing in and making a game-winning shot at the final buzzer

- Anytime a really old and beloved baseball player who is playing one of his last games gets a huge hit or makes a huge play

- Heartwarming moments between opponents (examples include: football players helping up a player who's been injured; anytime the losing side says extremely nice things about the winner; congratulations exchanged between Olympians from different nations because that is what the Olympics are all about, Louie says)

- Unlikely victories of any team, anywhere, but also

great competitive spirit shown by really unlikely teams (see: Jamaican bobsledding team in the 1988 Olympics, as in the movie *Cool Runnings*)

- A victory that arrives after all hope seems lost (see: the Chicago Cubs winning the World Series after a rain delay that arrived at the worst time—a moment when their opponents looked like they could take the lead—in the most dramatic game 7 ever!)

- Amazing plays (like mine) that happen just as the weather turns grim (like it did for mine!) in a game that had been extremely close (like mine!) up until that moment

In the ninth, I got on base and Devon hit a line drive to left that drove me home. We won the game easily, 2–0.

It was a **HUGE** game for me. **HUGE**. All-star material. I felt amazing. Diego **HAD** to be caught up in the emotions.

The only bummer was Johnny not being there to see it. I peered around in case he'd just moved when the rain started, but then I saw he had sent a text: "Sorry. Sasha drove me & had 2 get to her job and dropped me off first. But u were awesome!" (Smiley plus baseball glove emoji.)

No date request, but awesome was good, right?

The only other bummer was that as we packed up our things, Coach Hollylighter said, "Great pitching today, Gabby. You're the kind of person who can play anywhere on the field. Even catcher."

Meaning she was still thinking of me as a **CATCHER**.

MVP Summer Points: A solid 100, even if I won't be able to avoid future catcher duties

MVP Summer Tally: 540—I wonder if I should start thinking about what kind of medal to get myself??

A BRIEF TIME-OUT TO DISCUSS . . .

The Write-Up

So I was super excited to open the paper today and see what Diego had written.

But his article was . . . **FLAT**. Flatter than a basketball that's been deflated and then run over by a steamroller.

(I'd have used a baseball but baseballs don't get flat. I think they're the only sports ball that doesn't really. Okay, bowling and golf balls and lacrosse balls and softballs and, okay, I've proven basketball was the way to go.)

He talked about Mario's home run and, just to prove he wasn't flat about everything, he said about the hit, "Just as the game looked like it might head into a long set of extra innings, Salamida stepped up with a big swing to crank out a massive solo home run that thrilled the crowd."

THRILLED.

He talked about Alexander and I being a good matchup. And he'd avoided the part about me throwing my whole body over first base. Plus, he mentioned my double play, but there was no suspense, no drama, no excitement. He didn't even mention the **RAIN**! Just one line: "Catching a pop fly from Diaz, Garcia and teammate Devon Dewitt managed a double play." Managed? What, were we working at Louie's office now? How boring. Where was the weather and the tension and all the **THRILLING** things I had done?

I texted him. "Hey, thanks for coming to the game yesterday."

It was **THREE MINUTES** before he texted back. "I had to. For the paper."

Huh? Diego **LIKED** my games.

Then he added, "But I never miss your games, G!"

That was more like it.

"Did U C that bird on the backstop during your at bat? **A NELSON'S SPARROW?**"

He must have meant the bird that I got mad at. **OF COURSE** he meant the bird I got mad at.

"I don't think so."

"Yeah, they R usually super secretive so maybe that's why. Wish I could have been closer to hear its awesome **SONG**!"

Okay, I just had to act like this didn't bother me.

"Maybe next time U will. Hey! Do you want to ride bikes to see if we can find the Freezemobile? My treat!"

"Ugh, I have to write my birding column but Mom bought a ton of freeze pops! Do U want to come over?"

I did want to, but that wasn't MVP Summer material. And what if Diego ignored me the whole time because of his column? It would be me and a freeze pop and rejection. I needed to hang out with him when he wasn't distracted. Whenever that would be. "I should do some skydiving research. Will let U know what I find out."

I hoped that would intrigue him.

"Um, okay. Talk later!"

Bah. Skydiving got nothing?? Was Diego's head too far in the clouds looking for birds to see amazing things right in front of his eyes?

Or were we just not the same friends we used to be?

Gabby: Thx for coming 2 my game!

Johnny: Wish I could have stayed. Saw Diego's story.

(Ugh, what did that mean? Diego's story made the game sound like one no one would want to stay at.)

Gabby: Yep, me too. I saw your story on the new SoccerPlex. Cool!

Johnny: Now wkg on my math tutor column. Ugh, is that weird? A math column?

Gabby: No! It sounds helpful!

(Wanted to text: "Do I need hand-holding tutoring?" But I did not.)

Johnny: That's what Diego said. He gave me tips.

Gabby: Oh, that's nice u have a colleague.

(Wanted to text: "Did you give him a tip that his story was **FLAT**?")

Johnny: I was thinking of getting froyo tmrw. Wanna meet up?

Gabby: Sure!

(Meet up? What did that mean? Was that a date?)

Johnny: Swirl World @ 2?

Gabby: For swirl!

(Oh, no. Note to self: Double-think texts before typing them. But when in doubt, include a lot of emojis to make people forget what you typed.)

Gabby: 😊😊🌀🧁🧁😊😊😊🧁🧁🧁🧁

Johnny: 😊😊😊😊😊😊🧁🧁🧁🧁🧁🧁🧁

SLIDING INTO SECOND DATE (MEET-UP?)

MVP Summer Goal: Really get to know Johnny Madden!
MVP Summer Action: Unsure, because **I STILL DON'T KNOW WHAT A MEET-UP IS**!!

Post-Date Analysis:
June 30

After making sure that Peter had plans at least five miles away from Swirl World, I asked Louie to drive me to my "meet-up." I wanted Johnny to officially call it a date, but I was trying to come up with advantages to it being a meet-up.

FROYO MEET-UP VERSUS FROYO DATE

Meet-up: Breezy, friendly, totally no stakes. Get whatever flavor you want, even if you think it might make you barf! Gummy toppings that get stuck in your teeth are A-OK! Sit side-by-side and observe other people's yogurt-making habits!

Date: What do you even **SAY** when you get there? Stick to tried-and-true flavors because pickleberry sounds totally chancy. Consider all toppings for potential teeth-sticking or risk of food mustache. Sit across from each other and stare into eyes (?) or make brilliant conversation (???).

So I felt a little better. Except, could you hold hands on a meet-up? I hoped so. Then Louie started making it weird.

"So, have you told Diego about Johnny yet?"

I said, "Yeah, I told him the other day, during the bird thing."

"Was it . . . strange?"

"Why would it be . . . strange? I mean, except for the strange thing where Diego loves birds more than baseball now and he and Johnny already know each other and they both have junior reporter jobs at the *Peach Tree Gazette* but otherwise, why?"

"Oh, just I thought maybe Diego liked you. Like, liked you liked you."

EWW! GAH. NO!! AUGGGGGHHH! The only thing weirder than having a date would be having a date with Diego!

I must have said the **EWW! GAH!** noises in my head out loud because Louie smiled and said, "Well, it's not unheard of for friends to start to like each other."

"We do like each other," I told her. "But not like **THAT**." Between the birds and the flat story and not seeming that excited to MVP Summer it up with me, part of me wasn't sure if Diego liked me much at all. But for the purposes of **MY** MVP Summer (in other words, all the activities that didn't include Diego directly, like baseball games and Johnny . . . meet-ups), I couldn't think about that now.

"Okay, just checking," Louie said. "But you seem to have it figured out." How's that for a grown-up thing to say that drives kids (at least me) bananas??? I wasn't feeling like I had anything figured out lately.

THINGS GROWN-UPS SAY
THAT DRIVE KIDS BANANAS

- "You seem to have it figured out."

- "If I tell you what to do, how will you **LEARN**?"

- "What do you **WANT** to happen?" (If I knew, I wouldn't ask!)

- "Do you really think that's a good idea?"

But then we pulled up to Swirl World, where Johnny Madden was waiting on a bench outside. He was jotting things down in a notebook, which he always carried. I think he did math for fun, which made sense to me because why not actually enjoy what you're great at? Maybe it was key to him and Diego getting along. Diego is an expert at sports history (and sports around the world—like Hornussen), but Johnny was really into stats.

He looked up and waved and I said to Louie in one big breath, "That'sJohnnyandwe'regoingtohaveyogurtnowand I'lltextyouassoonasit'sdoneandpleasepickmeup. Thanks! Bye!"

And I sort of ran out of the car. Maybe with a little too much speed because I sort of tripped over the curb to the door of the store but I quickly recovered. I kept tripping over things! That was not **LIKE ME**. If Johnny could be even a fraction less cute, I might be a little more coordinated.

"Hi," I said to Johnny, out of breath from falling but also because his hair was messy in a kind of dreamy way. And mine was not in the braid he'd said he liked but then

166

he said, "You look nice," anyway, and the comment would have knocked the braid right out of my hair if I had worn it.

I went to hold a door open for Johnny, who was also trying to hold the other door for me, and then we both kind of walked in at the same time saying "thank you" like weirdos and then smushing into the store. And then he tripped a little! Did that mean I was cute enough to make him clumsy, too?

Our shoulders touched together and I thought for a second it was going to be hand-holding time but no, **UGH**. But I guessed we needed our hands to get yogurt. Also, it was much brighter in Swirl World than the movies and we'd be sitting face-to-face. What if I got sprinkles in my teeth?

The date yips (I guess there were yips for second dates, too, and meet-ups) were coming on full-fledged when

I saw a high school couple at the next table. They were feeding each other spoonfuls of yogurt in an extremely mushy way and exchanging kisses between spoonfuls. It was more uncomfortable than watching the romantic parts of a movie with your parents in the room. Johnny and I practically ran by their table like it was the scariest part of a haunted house.

The man at the register gave us little sample cups so we could try flavors before we got one. Those cups are disasters and I completely overfilled every one of them, and then I wound up getting what I always get, half banana, half cake batter. Sometimes I like to mix it up with a

special-edition flavor, but there was no room for anything
that might make me feel like
vomiting.

Johnny and I bumped
hands several times
when going for toppings,
because we liked the
same ones, which was a
good sign, but was also
making my legs all wobbly.

When we sat down and

FROZEN YOGURT
TOPPING COMPATIBILITY:
WE'RE A MATCH!
SPRINKLES
NUTS
COOKIE DOUGH
CHOCOLATE FUDGE
JOHNNY'S 4/4
MINE 4/4

ate our first spoonfuls, I took action. I would not allow us to
be all quiet and weird. "Did you finish your math column?
Did your sister get to work on time? What does she do?" I
wanted to ask about what Diego had said about the game,
but I didn't want to talk about Diego. Also, I had definitely
asked enough questions in a row.

"She's a counselor at an art camp for kids and they had
a show on Saturday," Johnny said. "And my math column
turned out okay but I'm excited because I got asked to
write a roundup on the high school soccer teams."

"Cool!" I said, hoping there weren't sprinkles in my
teeth. "How is that going?"

"Diego has been helping me get up to speed on local
sports stuff," Johnny said. "He knows *everything*. I wish I'd

met him sooner." Okay, so maybe *Johnny* was here to talk about Diego.

"I never knew you liked to write," I said, wondering if Johnny wished he'd met Diego before he met me. "I thought you were a numbers person."

He shrugged and smiled. "I always have been, but I wanted to try something new. Isn't everyone kind of an everything person, in a way?" He pointed at me. "Like you're a poetry person. And it seems like you're really good at getting everyone to like you."

Thank goodness yogurt melted in your mouth because I might have choked on mine otherwise! Did he mean HE liked me? That **HAD** to be what he meant.

Except then came this: "You and Diego have that in common, huh?"

NOOOOOO.

It was **FINE** Johnny and Diego were friends. Really.

But did that mean Johnny was asking me to do things because I was his friend's friend? Or were Johnny and I more than friends? I wished there was a Date Umpire who could call it.

DATE GOING WELL!

"I don't know about **EVERYONE** liking me or if they like me as much as they all like Diego," I said. Then I waited, thinking Johnny would get specific about his liking and of **WHOM** and hopefully **HOW**.

Nope. A **VERY AWKWARD SILENCE** seemed to melt over us.

So I pretended we never talked about that at all. "But on the thing you said, I think it's okay for people to be one **MAIN THING**," I said, hoping I sounded wise and crush-worthy. "Like, my favorite thing is baseball and then I have poetry and being too *everything* would make it hard, don't you think?"

"Well, sure," Johnny said. "But Diego was saying this interesting thing the other day about how he became a bird-watcher and how that's made him, like, **EXPAND** his idea of everything he can be. Like, what would you be if you were going to expand what you could be?"

I was out of yogurt. And I hadn't answered Johnny. "I would expand my yogurt to a second helping," I joked. "Do you want more?"

"For sure. I'm kind of full but I like talking to you," Johnny said, and he smiled. "Diego said his favorite thing to do since getting back from Costa Rica is mix coconut and dark chocolate. Should we try it?"

OMG. He liked talking to me. But then he'd brought up

Diego. Again! He wanted to stay. He kept smiling at me in a way that felt almost like hand-holding. The meet-up definitely wasn't a failure. But was it a **DATE**? Sigh. I knew we had one thing in common. Diego. Diego, who was the reason I wanted an MVP Summer in the first place, seemed to be the main reason I wasn't sure I was having one!

MVP Summer Points: 100 for overcoming the massive weirdness of a date, minus 50 for all the QUESTIONS it leaves me with!

MVP Summer Tally: 640

READING THE SIGNS

MVP Summer Goal: Get Diego to ask for **THE PLAN**
MVP Summer Strategy: **I DON'T KNOW! UGH, DIEGO!**

Post-Day Analysis:
July 2

Okay, so this is the point in Major League Baseball when teams reach the All-Star break. There's a game—National League versus American League—and a home run derby and all of it doesn't count so much but is a fun moment before everyone gets really **FIERCE** about which teams will make the playoffs. It's also when you kind of know who's looking great, who's falling short, etc. I knew my MVP Summer was stalled, or stalled on the pivotal Diego front at least. It wasn't great on the baseball front with the catching stuff, but I thought there was good progress on the Johnny front. But Diego: besides the sleepover and the game and a few random hangouts that were mostly watching baseball games at my house or his, we hadn't had a chance to do anything BIG. We were having a nice-enough summer but was it in the running to be an MVP Summer? I wasn't so sure.

Anytime I tried to pitch an idea, Diego had a birding thing or something to work on for the *Gazette* or **FAMILY** to see, and anytime he invited me anywhere, I had practice or, in the case of birding, an excuse for why I couldn't. I just wanted things to be exactly as they were before, when Diego would count on me for **THE PLAN**. But now he didn't seem to care about a plan at all. What had Costa Rica done to him? I had a mini golf coupon for buy one, get one putt-putt at Neptune's Back Nine, which was close enough to ride our bikes. Plus, we might even spy the Freezemobile, which meant ice cream. It wasn't totally MVP Summer material but I thought I'd take what I could get. So I texted him: "Wanna mini golf? Have a coupon!"

"Ugh," came Diego's reply. **NOT** what I was looking for. "That sounds fun but my mom is taking me to get new shorts because I outgrew mine."

Was that code? Was Diego actually outgrowing **ME**?

"Tomorrow?" he added.

"I have practice. But a game on the 4th. Catching. ☹"

"Oh! That's right! Sweet! 4th will rule!"

Definitely!

MVP Summer Points: Suspending awarding of points for All-Star break, which doesn't count anyway.

MVP Summer Tally: Holding at 640

GABBY AT HOME PLATE (A CATCHER'S SAGA IN THE STYLE OF THE FAMOUS POEM, "CASEY AT THE BAT"—BUT NOT THAT GOOD! I'M STILL GETTING THE HANG OF THIS!)

It was Fourth of July in Peach Tree and the heat was on . . . something was going to burst.

My forehead itched, my eyes were sweaty, playing catcher seemed like the worst.

But Coach said, "Hey, you have to, I think you don't know your own power."

And by now I knew better than to say, "Maybe, but boy do I need a shower."

So, down in the dirt I went, my face facing each opposing batter's butt,

I lifted my mitt and looked toward Casey, who'd gotten out of his pitching rut.

The stands were all full and my family was there, and so were Diego and dreamy Johnny.

I had to admit, I wanted a hit, because all of them had for sure come just to see me.

But for now I was catching, with a batter on base. My sign told Casey to hurl his most fast,

So he listened—he did!—and tossed with such speed that his first pitch went right past.

Past, yep, the batter but also past me and, ugh, this was an embarrassment!

The runner stole second and I couldn't peek at my friends but could feel the sad vibes that they sent.

It's okay, I regrouped, got my head in the game and the next pitch was a swing and miss.

I shot back to Casey and readied my glove, eager to put three outs on our list.

It wasn't so bad, at least for today, because I was really calling the shots.

I'd give a sign, Casey would nod, say it's fine, and strikes, he kind of threw lots.

I could see all the action from home plate, even from my catcher's crouch,

It wasn't so awful, after a while, almost like getting the best spot on the couch.

But Casey's arm grew tired in the seventh, and things began to look very grim . . .

With Devon at Disneyland and Alfonso at first, we had no pitchers to put in.

He loaded the bases, it was sad to say, but it just made me want to win more,
And then the next batter hit down the third base line, this game for sure wasn't a snore.
Mario grabbed for the ball. His runner broke for home plate . . .
But thwack! came the throw and I tagged the base: I got him out! It was great!

And then the day's good feeling was like sunshine, filling every possible space.
Things were so nice and all felt so right, as Diego's family invited us all to their place.
The Parkers' annual Independence Party was definitely the place to be,
Food and a pool and friends from the block, plus my best friend Diego and my crush Johnny!

I still had a list as long as my arm of things to make this summer the best,
But since today was a holiday, maybe it was okay to give it a rest.

Still, I thought to July 5th and the fun that'd await—
skydiving or at least water slides,
Instead of too-busy Diego and no mini golf and a bird hobby I
wish would just fly.

Fireworks bursting was maybe the moment when I could have
an MVP Summer declared,
But looking up at the sky with my friend and my boyfriend(?)
felt so very rare . . .
That I just leaned back on the blanket and told myself now
wasn't the time . . .
But the game and day so inspired me that here I am writing
this rhyme!

THE GREATS: EMILY DICKINSON
AMERICAN POET

Born: December 10, 1830

Died: May 15, 1886

From: Amherst, Massachusetts

Known for: Writing nearly 1,800 poems, even though she only published about 12 in her lifetime.

Why she's great: In a way, she made poetry her own sport by creating her own rules around punctuation and sometimes even her own punctuation—she liked dashes that weren't the same length and sometimes even vertical!

Odd fact: Even though she was a recluse and hid away from people (especially in her later years; sometimes, I can understand!), she loved being outside and grew hundreds of flowers, planted vegetables, and took care of fruit trees. They totally inspired her and she wrote about flowers in her poems!

Second odd fact: Definitely wouldn't have liked group texts.

Her excellent thoughts: "Hope is the thing with feathers that perches in the soul—and sings the tunes without the words—and never stops at all." A little bird-y but also INSPIRING.

GROUP TEXT →NEVER AGAIN
(DOCUMENTED HERE FOR HISTORICAL REASONS)

L   HEY, WHO'S GOING TO KATY'S
     CONCERT AT PEACH TREE MALL?

M   ME!

A   ME!

S   DEF GONNA BE THERE!

C   WOULDN'T MISS IT!

           WHO JUST SAID THOSE THINGS???   ME

M   MOLLY!

A   ARLO!

S   SOPHIA!

C   COLIN!

L   PUT OUR NUMBERS IN YOUR PHONE!
     (THIS IS LISA)

           OKAY! I'LL BE THERE TOO! SEE YOU
           ALL BY THE STAGE?   ME

L   YESSSSSS!

A   ♡👀👍🎉✨

M   🎵♡👌😎♡♡

C   😄👏👀🎤📷👍

THE GET 'EM ALL TOGETHER

MVP Summer Goal: Have Diego meet **ALL** my friends and unite everyone in my MVP Summer mission!

MVP Summer Action: Make everyone part of the same **TEAM**! (It's so obvious, I shouldn't even have to write it!)

Post-Day Analysis:
July 5

THIS WAS IT! Or, that was my attitude this morning. I thought for sure there was no way Diego could not be seized with MVP Summer spirit after today. In fact, when this day began, I had decided to bring everyone I knew in on my MVP Summer magic.

I think it was because I'd survived the group text. Kind

of. Before I had a phone, I thought group texts sounded fun, like a huddle, but now they seemed scary. There were no rules to the group text, like a game of tag where no one was It. But I was still upbeat: most of the Piper Bell talent squad was back in town and we were going to Katy's **CONCERT. I'D MADE HATS!** Katy was performing her song "Flip your Lid," my new fave because *lid* is another word for hat, as in baseball hat, and I was going to give everyone a hat to flip during the song. How could it not be a true MVP Summer moment with **HATS**?

And, after yesterday's awesome Fourth of July, I decided to call Diego and invite him. I wanted to invite Johnny, too, but I was still a little lost. He'd sat next to me on the fireworks blanket and I absolutely **FELT** fireworks but there was no hand-holding and that made me wonder: what if he was only at Diego's house for **DIEGO**? Definitely a possibility. So I was starting with Diego, my oldest best friend, and would work my way up to Johnny.

I called Diego, rather than text him. He answered, "Why are you calling?"

"Because they're still phones. That you can **TALK** into." Really, I didn't understand why I had to remind Diego of this. Or anyone. I felt a little abnormal about my reaction to sending and getting texts—because **EVERYONE** seemed to like them—but sometimes, they seemed like they took a completely easy thing (dial number, actually speak to the person you need to talk to, maybe even right away!) and made it a hard thing (send message, then either: wonder if person saw message/wonder if person saw message and is ignoring you/get message back, wait/wait/wait or type/type/type and be unsure if things are jokes or serious because you can't hear the other person's voice/and finally, think about all of these things way more than you ever thought about a phone call!). It was mentally exhausting on top of making my fingers cramp (and, as a pitcher, I could not have my fingers cramping).

TEXTING vs CALLING
(A GUIDE)

TEXTING

1. HARD TO TYPE PROPERLY UNLESS YOU HAVE TEENY FINGERS — NORMAL vs. NORMAL FINGERS

2. DANGER OF EMBARRASSING SPELLING MISTAKE....

3. HARD TO MAKE JOKES FUNNY (LOL?)

4. WHAT IF THE SMILEY EMOJI YOU USED ISN'T THE RIGHT SMILEY EMOJI??? ☺ OR ☺ OR ☺

5. WAITING FOREVER FOR THE RESPONSE
   (NOTE: IN TEXTING 30 SECONDS CAN SEEM LIKE FOREVER!)

CALLING

1. ⟩NO TYPING AT ALL⟨ JUST USE YOUR MOUTH TO TALK AS NORMAL — Hi!

2. ALSO NO SPELLING (UNLESS SPECIFICALLY REQUESTED!)

3. IF YOU'RE JOKING, THE PERSON CAN HEAR IT IN YOUR VOICE!

4. SMILES ALSO TRANSMIT OVER PHONE

5. IN LONG PAUSE, YOU CAN ASK, "ARE YOU STILL THERE?"

Texting sometimes feels like a sport I'm not good at. It wasn't a feeling I was used to, and I didn't like it one bit.

"Yeah, I guess I wish there were more bird emojis. They seem underrepresented," Diego said. "But I like texting better than calling." The statement made my chest hurt a little since I was on the phone with him. Before Costa Rica, Diego and I had agreed on everything, but now he was Mr. Bird Lover and a Fan of Texting and, maybe a little bit, less of a Fan of Gabby.

"I thought we could all go see Katy perform at the mall. Some of the other talent squad members are going and I thought then you could meet everyone. It might be fun," I said and waited. I was nervous.

"Oh, cool! Johnny and I were talking about going to that so we can write something for the *Gazette*," Diego said. "So then we'll see you there!"

Wait . . . what? Now Diego and Johnny were making plans without me? So maybe Johnny **WAS** at Diego's house on the Fourth of July just for Diego. What if he'd wished I hadn't been there at all? **BUT** there were all the good signs, like saying I looked nice and our yogurt-topping compatibility and all the smiling and tripping over things. Plus, I had this feeling that when my insides went all cotton candy, Johnny's were doing the same thing. Still, I'd had a feeling at the regional game that we'd win and we hadn't. I'd been wrong about Diego's enthusiasm for MVP Summer activities. Ugh. What if I was wrong about **EVERYTHING**?

Bob: *Wow, has Gabby been totally shut out of the Diego–Johnny friendship?*

Judy: *Bob, I think that's a little off base. Diego and Johnny work together and of course they're going to hang out sometimes.*

Bob: *I don't know. I think she has a reason to call foul.*

Judy: *I think she should see how today goes first.*

Okay, so maybe Diego and Johnny were friends because of the paper, but that was normal. And I should have been glad they were getting along. Just, why did they have to get along without **ME**?

"I'll be with all my friends. From the talent squad. We got pretty close while I was at Piper Bell," I said, blurting it out because I felt the slightest twinge of jealousy. But it was true: my new friends were a talent squad who did things, not just a bunch of bird-watchers who had to stand completely still. Still, I hated the ugly cloudy feeling I had.

"Great!" Diego said. "I can't wait to meet them! Johnny and I will meet you at the mall. You know, play it by ear."

I agreed to play it by ear even though I wanted to have a **PLAN**! Like, where exactly would we meet and what did they want to do after and how did I fit in to the Diego-Johnny friendship and did Johnny like me like me and if yes, why hadn't he and Diego **ASKED ME**?

Also, I'd forgotten to mention the **HATS**!

But okay. I made it to the mall. By car, not by ear! And, well, there were lots of other people arriving. I realized that while it was **AWESOME** to have Katy sing the National Anthem before the Braves game, at that event, everyone was really there to see the Braves. The crowd at the Peach Tree Mall was all there for **HER**.

And the crowd was **GIGANTIC**.

How had I wound up friends with someone who could get a billion people to come to her concert? (Okay, not a billion, but **A LOT**. Like the mall version of a billion. I can decide on things like that because I have poetic license.) I tried to calm the mini Gabbys who started to freak that they wouldn't find anyone and would just be carrying around a bunch of hats with no heads to put in them!

The show was in the middle of the mall's Sun Court with a big stage set up where normally there's a Jamba Juice stand. They'd moved Jamba Juice for **KATY**! Despite being worried I wouldn't find the squad or Diego and Johnny, I started to get excited for her.

THINGS THAT ARE A BIG DEAL

- Anytime my little brother says something nice to me before he's fully awake and realizes what he is saying. (Things that count as nice include "Excuse me," "Can you please pass the syrup?" "Good game"—must be a dream game since he never says that after my **ACTUAL GAMES**.)

- Batting .350 or above. (The phrase "batting a thousand" is just silliness because even the **VERY BEST** batters are only going to bat a thousand if they've only been at bat a few times. If you're up to bat and you are swinging, then hitting 30 percent or more of the pitches is a **BIG DEAL**! Glad I cleared that up. For myself.)

- Real ice cream (I can never admit this to others but even though froyo is great, I am much more excited about real ice cream, especially when I get to eat it out of a tiny Braves baseball hat.)

- Pitching a no-hitter. (Even if Life MVPs are modest, this is my playbook and I can say freely here that my no-hitter history is a **BIG DEAL**!)

- Any event that forces Jamba Juice to move!

Anyway, I was weaving through a crowd of a million people and even though I could see the stage, I couldn't see where the crowd ended. And with everyone just playing it by ear, we'd all agreed to meet at the concert. We'd all assumed that the concert was going to be like a school play or

something. **NOT A JAMBA-JUICE-NEEDS-TO-GET-OUT-OF-THE-WAY EVENT!**

Anyway, I was lost among the billions of Katy fans and, even if I don't like to admit it, I'm not very tall. (Despite me being older, Peter is as tall as me, and it seemed that I was below-average height for a Katy Harris concertgoer.)

When I kept seeing unfamiliar faces, I started to sweat. To my left was a circle of girls about my age in homemade T-shirts that said "See the Day," and to my right was a group of teenagers—actual teenagers who probably could drive and go wherever they wanted but had chosen to see

MY FRIEND perform and I wanted to say **I KNOW HER!** But I didn't see anyone I **KNEW**.

But then . . .

"Hey, Gabby!" came Molly Oliver's voice to my left!

"Gabby, over here!" came Diego's and Johnny's voices to my right!

My friends were **TALL**! And they'd spotted me. But who to go to first? It was my dilemma, but in a not-just-in-my-head and completely **REAL** way. I kind of wanted to show Diego that I was super important to the talent squad by going to them first, but I also thought that would be kind of a rude move since part of inviting Diego was to get our MVP Summer ball really rolling, as **BEST FRIENDS**. I stood frozen on the spot.

I shuffled sideways toward Molly and the gang—Arlo, Sophia, Colin, Marilyn, Lisa, Arnold —and heard Diego, standing with Johnny, say, "No, Gabby, we're over here!"

I knew it didn't actually **MATTER** which group I picked. But I also didn't **WANT** to choose.

"Come get your hats, guys!" I held the bag of baseball caps up in the air and waved it around: the solution to my problem! I was a genius!

"Gabby, are you okay . . . you're really **RED**," Diego said as he and Johnny approached. It wouldn't have been a big deal if it were just me and him but I felt like him saying it was just drawing attention to my **SWEATINESS**. Especially when no one else looked red, and Johnny, who was the first to put on a hat—a **GOOD SIGN**—looked breezy and easy and not **SWEATY**.

"It's just . . . it's hot. And I was looking for you guys and . . ."

"Why didn't you just text if you couldn't find us?" Molly asked.

TEXT! Why didn't I think of that?? What good was a phone if you forgot you had it when it could actually be useful!

"These are awesome," Johnny said, tipping the brim of his hat. "Are you just good at everything?"

OMG. I felt like the mall had moved Jamba Juice to make room for my beating **HEART**! Maybe Johnny would have come to **SEE ME**, even if he didn't have an assignment with Diego.

"Thank you," I said to him and the whole time I was imagining a different version of the moment where I walked in unsweaty and not frazzled.

Then I pretended I was wearing my mitt and holding a baseball and a very pitcher-like idea came to me: to just be the center. So I said, "Hey, everyone, this is Diego. He just got back from Costa Rica and he works with Johnny at the *Gazette* for the summer. Diego, this is everyone. Well, not the whole squad, but some very important members."

That was good, I thought, accentuating everyone's importance.

"Whoa, Costa Rica!" Molly said. "I've always wanted to go! My family just got back from Peru. We climbed Machu Picchu."

"Wow, I didn't know you were going there," Johnny said. "What were the views like?"

Meanwhile, Sophia and Arnold had started to talk to Diego—about his necklace of all things. Sophia said it really "shredded." And Arnold, who was a drama king (he's an actor), started asking about whether Diego had lived in a hut. And then there were two conversations going on between excited groups and . . .

No one was talking to me exactly but that was okay, because I'd been the **UNITER** and that would get the **FUN** started. Then, as if to amp up the fun

I'd launched, a set of rainbow lights flashed over the crowd and a voice boomed over the mall loudspeakers.

"AND NOW, PEACH TREE MALL WOULD LIKE TO WELCOME OUR CITY'S VERY OWN SINGING SENSATION . . . KATY . . . HARRIS!!!"

If I thought it was loud before, the sound of the crowd cheering felt loud enough to lift my feet right off the floor. And then there was Katy, in the middle of a cloud of blue fog, and a glittery curtain came down behind her as she started to sing "See the Day," the song she'd done on TV. The entire crowd turned to face the stage as if they'd practiced how to do it and in moments we were all singing along and jumping up and down.

In the middle of my friends, jumping around, I felt **GREAT**. Like being on the mound in the thick of the action: everyone was smiling and winning and wearing our hats and it was because of me!

Katy. **WAS. AMAZING.** "How are you guys doing today, Peach Tree??? I'm so excited to be here!" The way she said it, there was no way it was anything but one hundred thousand percent true.

"Yeah, Katy!" I cheered and then our little team started a chant, **"KA-TY, KA-TY, KA-TY."** And then the **WHOLE CROWD** joined in.

She performed about six more songs and did "Flip Your Lid" as an encore. A big screen came down because the song also featured dance moves she'd created. None of our crowd except for Sophia was very good at them yet but with the hats, we made up a move where we actually flipped the cap on backward while we kind of faked knowing the steps.

FLIP YOUR LID

Today was a no-go
Your vibe was a no-show
Wanna crawl back in bed
Watch the world go by instead
But you gotta/But you gotta/But you gotta

Flip your lid
Get your head on right
Turn things around
Don't give up the fight
Nobody seems to get you
Doing the things that you do
But you can't give up the you you are
Your life is yours, you're the star
So you gotta/you must/you will
Flip your lid
Get your head on right
Turn things around
Don't give up the fight
So flip your lid if you need to
Turn things over 'cause you're going to
Get it right the right way
As long as you just be you

Then, **MASSIVE APPLAUSE** and it couldn't have been better. It was like we were all sharing the Katy glow. "Thank you all! Especially my friends over there!" And she pointed right at **US**! I thought I saw her flash Diego a massive smile.

We couldn't go talk to her because she was surrounded by a crowd of fans who wanted her to sign things. Then the mall manager came out to say Jamba Juice would be back tomorrow. When things quieted down, we all chattered about how great the show was.

Everyone had left their hats on and we totally looked and felt like a team. Diego seemed to fit right in and was having a good time and so was Johnny. I started to plan what we would all be doing the rest of the summer.

"We're going for milkshakes. You're coming, right?" Molly asked me.

"Yeah, definitely," I said. Over milkshakes, I'd tell everyone we'd scored **MASSIVE POINTS** on the way to an MVP Summer! I looked at Diego and Johnny. "Let's go!"

"Oh, um, we're going over to the Sports Barn," Diego said. "Did you know two former Olympians work there? A fencer and a trapeze artist? We're profiling the hidden super-athletes in town."

The Sports Barn is an old barn that runs all kinds of clinics and classes for kids, mostly little ones. How many stories were they writing for the *Gazette*? And couldn't they go some other time?

"We were thinking you might want to go, too," Johnny said, but it was clear "you" just meant me and not **ALL OF US**. **UGH!** Of course I wanted to go! But I wanted **EVERYONE** to go somewhere **TOGETHER**. We were a **TEAM**! We'd just had a total MVP Summer Moment and I'd helped make it and now everyone was **SPLITTING UP**!

"Oh, well, you guys have to get your story, so, um, I'll just go for milkshakes." Even though I felt like someone had tossed my lid on the ground and stomped on it, everyone else was completely casual as we said our goodbyes and went off in different directions. **AGAIN.**

I'd managed to get my friends together for **ONE PLAY**, but that wasn't going to win the game, much less the **SUMMER**.

MVP Summer Points: 100 for good vibes, minus 40 for giving up the win.

MVP Summer Tally: 700

PLAYING IT BY EAR,
A POEM BY GABBY GARCIA

We can play it by ear
Is something you hear
When everything is shaky
And weird.

Out on the field
The rules are all sealed
The game might by tough
But you're sure.

I can throw a baseball
So fast you can't see it at all
And hit a pitch
Over the fence.

So why can't my life
Be minus this strife?
I'd like some plans that are
Clear and concrete.

To make it clear:
It seems only fair
To make things more certain
Instead of just blurting,
"Let's play it by ear."

EVERYTHING HAS A CATCH

MVP Summer Goal: Play catcher like I was born to do it
MVP Summer Action: Overcome a case of the jerks (a trophy would help)

Post-Day Analysis:
July 8

So, maybe part of why I've struggled with the MVP Summer is that it's hard to have one when you're finding it hard to feel like an MVP yourself. First, there's Diego just seeming to want to flit around, all bird-obsessed and floaty and like my plans don't matter or even **OCCUR** to him. Then there's Johnny, who I like **SO MUCH** but what if he only likes me **SO MEH**? And, yeah, there's this whole catcher thing. I've had some good games—we've only lost one, and not even horribly!—but today I wanted to be pitching.

No such luck: Alfonso was back from his vacation and he was ready to go at pitcher. I didn't even have a shot at reliever because Casey's confidence had gotten a boost after the Fourth of July game.

This meant that Devon and I were keeping the positions that were not our positions.

"But we won our first game because Gabby pitched," Devon was saying to Coach Hollylighter and Coach Daniels.

"Yeah, and shouldn't switching up our positions include also switching **BACK** to our **REAL** positions?" I added, to back her up.

Coach Hollylighter wasn't having it. "Look, I know you're not crazy about this arrangement, but we're not doing it just to torture you."

"For the love of the game, you need to think of **EVERY** position as your real position," Coach Daniels said. "I stand by Coach Hollylighter." He was doing a lot of that lately.

We took warm-ups with Alfonso on the mound and me, covered in heavy gear, crouching behind home plate. We were the away team, playing at a different field than our practice spot and our usual field. So **FAR AWAY**, in fact, that no one but Louie and my dad even came to the game. The sun was in my eyes. And the dirt that blew up in my face with each little burst of wind seemed itchier than our practice field's dirt.

I wasn't having a case of the yips. I was having a case of the jerks.

I knew I was being a jerk. All my little Gabbys were sitting down and pouting and more or less saying, "What are you gonna do about it?" to me the whole game.

I'd never really had a case of the jerks for a baseball game before.

CASES OF THE JERKS, DOCUMENTED BY GABBY

- On my tenth birthday, when Diego had to go to his cousin's graduation party and my parents took me to the movies but the movie I wanted was sold out and I had to see Peter's movie instead

- The weekend when Dad experimented with health pancakes

- The time, as a nine-year-old Little Leaguer, I drew the short straw and had to dress in a turtle costume (our team mascot) for the Peach Tree Parade

There were other examples. But basically, the jerks were different from the yips because the yips were nervousness and being scared to do a thing because you wanted to do the thing so badly, while the jerks came from *not* wanting to do a thing. **AT. ALL.** Even if you try to psych yourself up, you can't, because the jerks won't budge.

But the game had to go on. So I trudged to home plate in the eight thousand pounds of gear. Really, what was I learning by having to trudge to a position I didn't play?

Alfonso gave up a home run in the **FIRST INNING**.

I needed motivation to keep at this catching thing but I wasn't finding it anywhere. And, with my case of the jerks, I wasn't even **TRYING** to find it. It wasn't like Johnny or Diego were there to even see me in full jerks mode, so the only witnesses were my parents, who had to love me no matter what. I was so jerky I wanted to high-five the other team's batter as she crossed home, but instead I lifted my mask and saw Devon at shortstop, shaking her head moodily. At third, Mario was kicking the base, as if he was angry at it for existing. I knew the feeling.

At least my case of the jerks was not limited to just me.

In the top of the fourth, when we were at bat and I thought I might have sweated out most of my brain, Coach Hollylighter gathered us around. We were down, but only 2–1, by some miracle. I had to admit, Alfonso's fastball was pretty good, and pretty fast, even if it hurt my hand to catch it. Some of his luck, I thought, had to do with the team: we were playing Sylvester, two towns over, who were maybe not quite all-stars.

"I know we're all trying out best out there, right, team?" Coach Hollylighter looked at us meaningfully. It takes a while in life to know when a grown-up is looking at you meaningfully, but once you know the signs, you never stop noticing it.

SIGNS OF A GROWN-UP GIVING YOU A MEANINGFUL LOOK

- Usually occurs after a question you know you have the wrong answer to (Are you trying your hardest/doing your best/thinking that's a good idea/happy with yourself/etc.?)

- Look is often accompanied by a long pause

- Head often tilts to one side, as if you are being examined but only casually

- Sometimes is interrupted by a quick look at the grown-up's hand, as if this might be more interesting than your meaningful answer

Everyone kind of murmured a "yes," except Alfonso, who really was giving it his best and said **"YES!"** in a much more excited way. Something about the way he said it made me think that I should do a little better for him. If he were catching for me, I'd want that.

Fine. I would have definitely wanted that. But I couldn't shake the jerks. Until . . .

I'm writing this post-game but here's a weird thing: when I made my MVP Summer Action plan about playing like there was a trophy, well, it was an imaginary trophy. Because the all-star league was new, the rules were still being sorted when it formed. **BUT THEN:**

"You know, I didn't mention this, but maybe I should," Coach Hollylighter said. "Our record is pretty good and despite the way I can tell some of you don't want to be here"—she looked right at me and Devon and Mario for sure—"the Atlanta-area team with the best record after seven games will win trophies."

TROPHIES! Okay, so I'd learned not to make everything about winning, but since the MVP Summer isn't exactly rocketing toward the Hall of Fame, I sure feel like I could use a trophy.

I looked at Devon and Mario and could see the trophy gleam in their eyes, too. I tried to send a telepathic message: "Dump the jerks, get a **TROPHY.**" And so I went back out there, still sweaty and uncomfortable but deciding that if I couldn't be center of the action at pitcher, I would be Alfonso's guide. I'd be the catcher I always dreamed of having. Hey! That's a pretty good idea. It's too bad I can't clone myself to be my own **IDEAL** catcher.

I picked up the pace of throwing the ball back to Alfonso, and when I had a good idea for a pitch to throw that I knew Alfonso could manage—he was good at

fastballs but also his curve was improving—I gave him a sign. A one-finger point for a fastball, or two for a curve. And he usually didn't wave me off. A couple times he did and, okay, those couple times he wasn't all wrong.

After those early innings when he wasn't top-notch, he was suddenly what we pitchers call being **ON FIRE**. (Really, the phrase should be for catchers, because a person really burns up in all this equipment on a Georgia summer day.)

As Alfonso's innings got better and better on the mound, we all did better and better at bat. By the seventh inning, we'd scored **FIVE** runs. Alfonso even got a double. He was pumped. The game, I had to admit, was **HIS**. The win, which we got, was **HIS**.

"Thanks for backing me up out there," he said to me as we left the field after the last inning. He offered me a hand to help me stand up. My hair was plastered to my head and my knees were shaky, so I gladly took the assist.

I wasn't used to backing anyone up, necessarily. I was used to **HAVING BACKUP**. But this summer was showing me that a lot of what I was used to wasn't what would happen. So, for today at least, I guessed I could live with letting Alfonso be the center of the victory. And so I said, "You're welcome." And he was.

MVP Summer Points: 50 (points lost for weak jerks start but an inspiring finish!)

MVP Summer Tally: 750—need to rack up some points but things are looking up!!

MUSICAL INTERLUDE

Katy and I finished our song—by text! It's a musical miracle!!

♪ ♫ Wanna Be an MVP ♫ ♪
by Katy Harris and Gabby Garcia

It's not easy
Trying to get this life thing right
So many ways to play it
☀ Morning, noon, and night. ☾

I may not bat one thousand
But I swing big every time ⚾
I may not get it perfect
But I still wanna climb ↗

209

I wanna be bigger than me/
Most Valuable Person
An MVP
It's not for the glory, it's not for the fame
But so you think good things when you hear my name

What makes you a winner
Isn't the points you score
What makes you a winner
Is inside, something more
Look my way and I'll smile ☺
Ask for help and I'll lend a hand
It can't be all about me
It's about good for my fellow human

I wanna be bigger than me/
Most Valuable Person
An MVP
♪ It's not for the glory, it's not for the fame
♫ But so you think good things when you hear my name

But after we hashed out the song, she sent this text: "How is **DIEGO**?" Because it seemed like even the people who liked me liked Diego more—with his many bird events and bird friends and his bird column in the paper and his **DIEGO-NESS** being shared with everyone but me. I guess that would have been easier to handle if we were our usual Gabby-and-Diego pair. Or even Diego-and-Gabby. But we were Diego (long pause) and (long pause) Gabby. He felt farther away now than he had in Costa Rica.

I said, "He's good." He was; he'd been over for dinner because his mom and dad had to work late and everything was fine. Or fine-ish. He gobbled down some of dad's ceviche and pretty much all of a bag of chips and then went on and on about a family of birds with a nest outside the offices to the *Gazette* and **BARELY** asked me about my game. (Okay, that's not true, he'd been pretty interested in the game, but I made a big deal about having to send Katy rhymes for the song because I was kind of stung by the bird thing.)

Then Katy asked if maybe we could all hang out, "Me, you, Johnny, and Diego." And knowing she like liked Diego reminded me that I **LIKED** Diego and today maybe I had been kind of having a case of the jerks with him, even if he didn't realize it. But a double date (or a double meet-up, if they have those) would be a way to do something nice for everyone. And maybe the moment I'd been waiting for!

Putt-Putt Perfection

MVP Summer Goal: Do something nice for Katy, and maybe putt our way to an MVP Summer moment I can celebrate

MVP Summer Action: A double date (will that get double **POINTS**?)

Post-Day Analysis:
July 11

Here's the thing: I wanted Diego to **WANT** to hang out with me. Since he'd gotten back, he wasn't sending signals that he **DIDN'T** want to, but things were different. I kept waiting for a moment when he asked, "What's the plan?" Or when I'd feel like he was backing me up in my quest for summer excellence. And the moment never came.

What if the part of Diego that thought Gabby Garcia

was the coolest friend ever hadn't come back from Costa Rica? Was that what had happened, or had I just been a bad friend to him when he was gone? It wasn't the kind of thing I could just ask him. Diego and I didn't argue, and I didn't want to accuse him of anything. Now, since Katy had asked me for a favor, I wanted to do something nice for her, and probably for Diego, too. I thought if I worked some first-date magic for them, I'd be Diego's hero again.

So, my brilliant idea was to play mini golf. It's the great equalizer of sports. Unlike regular golf, mini golf is **NOT BORING**. Mini golf is everything golf should be. Because it has diversions. And if there's one thing golf needs, it's diversions. Like, instead of a big huge field of

REGULAR GOLF | MINI GOLF

WIDE-OPEN BOREFEST...

OBSTACLE-FILLED EXCITEMENT!

grass between the tee and the hole, what if there were ramps and castles and places where a golfer hit into a mystery chute and didn't know where the ball would come out? Much more exciting. Plus, I knew Diego was really good at mini golf, so I'd be setting him up to **LOOK GREAT** for Katy. It was kind of **FUN**, planning it.

It was also kind of fun to be the one asking Johnny out. Why hadn't I thought of this before? I knew girls asked boys out all the time—we weren't dinosaurs!—but since the whole hand-holding-then-not incident, and the meet-up thing, and my wondering if he only even hung out with me because of Diego, I had hesitated. So I was casual in my text and said, "Katy said we should all get together, you, me, her, and Diego. I thought mini golf. You in?" I didn't call it a date or a meet-up. **PERFECT**. And he said **YES** and sent a series of emojis that included a guy and a girl standing next to each other. However, who knew

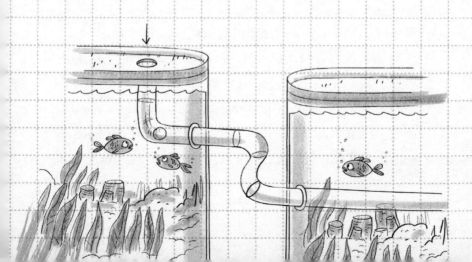

if they were on a date or just meeting up, because they weren't holding hands. (Note to self: ask emoji people for clear translations.)

Katy, Diego, Johnny, and I went to Neptune's Back Nine, an underwater-themed mini golf course. I rode with Diego to meet up with Katy and Johnny. "Thanks for setting this up, Gabs," he said, looking across the mini-van seat. "I'm really excited." **YES**! I thought. Diego was excited. A prime MVP Summer emotion!

When we walked up, Katy and Johnny were waiting with clubs. "They just gave them to us, because Katy's famous," Johnny said. And Katy looked totally embarrassed but maybe a little happy with herself. I understood.

"I like your shoes," Johnny said to me about the red high-tops I wore almost all the time.

"I like your tie," I said about the tie Johnny wore almost all the time.

We grinned at each other. "Are you sure your little brother's not here to heckle us?" Johnny peered over his shoulder. We had an **INSIDE JOKE**.

"Don't worry, I have a plan if he shows up," I said. I didn't, but this sounded good.

"I'm going to feel really pathetic if I have to run away from an eight-year-old," Johnny joked and I slapped my forehead and said "Darn it!" and then we smiled at each other and

Johnny tried to kind of toss and catch his club but dropped it. That had to be cotton-candy-feeling related, I thought.

Diego and Katy were standing to one side with their clubs, sort of nervous and watching this.

Johnny and I were **OLD PROS** at going out (except for the part where I was **VERY UNCLEAR** on if he would **EVER HOLD MY HAND AGAIN**) and Katy and Diego were sort of shy and fumbling around each other. They were having a conversation about different places where they'd mini golfed before, but they needed the action of the game to keep them from stalling, I could tell.

"Hey, it's our turn," I pointed out, and I could see relief on Diego's face. Johnny insisted I go first since I set every-thing up. On the first hole, you had to get your ball past an octopus whose arms moved to block it. I swung and a tentacle whacked my ball right back at me. It sent us all into giggle fits, which seemed to be like a breath of oxygen. Group laughter was definite MVP material. We relaxed more, commenting on each other's shots. I wasn't even worried about my score.

Katy, though, was an excellent scorekeeper, and I could tell she liked having something to do, plus a reason to talk to Diego. "Diego, was that two? You made par **AGAIN**." Diego beamed and gave me a thumbs-up. I had that pitcher-ness from Katy's show again, like I was the center of a very important game. But the neat thing was, everyone had a chance to be the star.

Like on the fourth hole, where you sent your ball down a ramp and then through a glass case where **REAL FISH** swam behind a series of pipes that your ball slid down, Diego scored a hole in one.

At hole eight, which had a bunch of banks and pits, Johnny knelt down and pointed out a few key details. "So, I think the trick is to hit **THAT** corner and then it will bank over to that curved part and **SHOULD** make it just under Neptune's feet," he told us, and the trick worked for Katy and Diego and Johnny, who all made par, but then I hit my ball too hard and it popped into the air, hit a prong on Neptune's trident, ricocheted back down, and went **RIGHT INTO THE HOLE**!

PHYSICS ⹂AND⹆ ATHLETICISM MEET!

"That. Was. Crazy. I've never seen anything like that,"
Johnny exclaimed, looking at me like I was a math miracle.
He ran his hands through his hair, which left him looking
like a mad scientist. **A CUTE ONE.**

"That was truly awesome, GG! Like, that ball had
MOVES!" Katy squealed.

"That's Gabby," Diego said. "She's the coolest."

"Thanks, Diego," I said, feeling really happy by his
compliment.

I had that peaceful sense of
getting everything right.
My friends were happy,
and I was responsible.
This was what it meant
to be an MVP. It was
almost as good as pitching a
no-hitter. No, it *was* as good.

Okay, all my friends were getting along perfectly, without me
having to do a thing. Maybe I wasn't responsible for anything other than picking out the color of my golf ball? Or
maybe, it was **MOMENTUM**. If I suggested some other
fun thing, the next MVP Summer moment would be on
the schedule.

"We should do something again soon," I said. "Like

next week, maybe we can go cosmic bowling! And maybe to the water park for the weekend!" If they said yes, I thought, I'd fill them in on the MVP Summer.

And everyone said, "It sounds great!" And I was about to formally announce MVP Summer, but then Diego said something about how he had to check his bird schedule and Katy had a rehearsal and Johnny said, "We definitely should do those things but I know there's a Calculus Camp tournament soon."

"We can pick other days . . ." I trailed off. It seemed time to lock something in. The summer was more than half over!

But everyone had begun talking—happily—about all their **OTHER PLANS**. Not worrying about our group momentum **AT ALL**. Diego looked at me and, trying to sound reassuring, said, "We'll figure it out, though, Gabs. 'Cause it would be fun."

As I write this before bed, with no next plan on the horizon, I feel a little like an almost-MVP whose season got cut short.

MVP Summer Points: 90 at first tee but subtract 20 for no follow-up

MVP Summer Tally: 820

BAD DAD JOKES YOU WILL HEAR A MILLION TIMES IF YOU FEEL DOWN

- Hey, Gabby, did you hear the one about the tissue that liked to dance? Yeah, it had a little boogie in it!

- Gabs, I think I must have dreamt I was a car muffler last night. I woke up **EXHAUSTED**!

- I read a statistic today . . . it's amazing. Do you know five-quarters of people are bad with fractions??

- What did the cheese say as it was being shredded? I don't feel so **GRATE**!

Dear Ms. Garcia and Family,

We are extremely pleased to extend to you an offer to attend Piper Bell Academy on a full scholarship for the coming academic year. After your excellent athletic and improving academic performance as a guest student, we hope you will consider continuing your studies and endeavors with us.

If you accept, please contact our enrollment offices no later than August 7. We look forward to your response.

Sincerely,

The Piper Bell Admissions Board

PICK THE PICKLE YOU PICKED

MVP Summer Goal: Say yes to Piper Bell! Immediately!
MVP Summer Action: Tell Diego I won't be going to Luther
(NOW he'll DEFINITELY want to pack what we have
left of summer with fun! Right?)

Post-Day Analysis:
July 14

In baseball, a pickle is what happens when you're stranded
between two bases. Maybe the batter hit a pop fly and
you started to run to second but the batter is out and the
ball is thrown to second, where the baseman waits to tag
you out, so you turn and run back to first and the second
baseperson throws to first and then the first baseperson
is waiting to tag you out. You could go back and forth

between the bases for a while. It's also called a rundown, but I like the term "pickle."

After I was done happy-dancing—a scholarship was HUGE!—I realized I was in a pickle.

My pickle was being caught between Diego and Piper Bell.

I was thinking of Piper Bell as a person almost. She was, actually: Piper Bell had founded the school after running a successful peach orchard. She could also fly planes and she built one of the area's first libraries, plus she wanted to create Renaissance students. That meant students who excelled in multiple fields, which was the reason the talent squad existed.

And the idea that someone as amazing as Piper Bell had sent me a letter to say, please, stick with me!—well, that felt important. Luther was the school I'd gone to my whole life and I loved it, but Piper Bell was a BIG DEAL. Their baseball team was better. Their facilities were better. There was the talent squad and an atrium and a massive school library. Plus, I'd already gone there, so I knew that it wasn't as terrifying as a private school might sound to an outsider.

I hadn't been expecting to love it as much as I had, but I did. I knew I wanted to go.

In my pickle, Piper Bell was the same as me advancing

to second. Sliding victoriously as the second baseperson narrowly missed tagging me out, actually.

But then I wouldn't be with Diego. Just those six months he was in Costa Rica had made him a totally different Diego! If we went to separate schools, would we even recognize each other in a year? He'd always been right there for me. I don't want to say he was my sidekick, but he'd always backed me up, no matter what. So if I picked a new school, would he still back me up?

Bob and Judy had a lot to say about it.

BOB   JUDY

≡ INSIDE GABBY'S BRAIN ≡

Bob: *Well, this is the true Gabby and Diego friendship moment, isn't it?*

Judy: *Bob, I'm in complete agreement. How Diego reacts will set the tone for everything else to come. I'm putting my bet on him being quite upset.*

Bob: *Why? He hasn't been upset about any other changes.*

Judy: *But this is the big one. It's going to matter.*

In the kitchen, Dad was already at work on a cake to celebrate. "It's the Scholar-Poet-Athlete!" he said as I walked in.

"Shouldn't it be Scholar-Athlete-Poet?"

"Then you're a SAP, and a SPA is better, don't think?"

Dad and Louie had of course assumed I'd be taking the scholarship. They were ready to join the Piper Bell Parents Club and buy Piper Bell gear and volunteer for everything. But I wasn't ready yet.

It was a super-hot day. So hot practice had been canceled. I texted Diego. "R U bird-watching today?"

"Wanted 2 but 2 **HOT**!"

"Want to go to the Lazy River with me?"

Louie was already taking Peter to Rip Tide Water Park, so I knew it would be no problem tagging along. And the heat was perfect; if Diego actually had nothing else to do for once, he'd be in. "Sounds great," he texted back quickly. Knew it!

I had it all planned out. We'd have a totally relaxing day, drinking slushies and staying cool, and then I'd tell him.

Every overheated birder in town was at the water park when we arrived. No less than five people said hi to Diego and said they were bummed he'd canceled a birding expedition. Diego just shrugged and said "Definitely soon" and introduced me to everyone, forgetting some of them had sort of met me the day the bird pooped on me. He seemed to want to hang with me the **MOST**. A good sign.

"Watch out for a special delivery from above," said the girl who'd shushed me for my snacks. But it didn't bother me.

"It's a lot of work keeping the bird crowd happy," Diego said to me as we walked away. "I was really looking forward to just relaxing today. Can you believe school starts in a month? Someone asked if I'm going to do a birding club at Luther. I mean, it sounds great, but I just want to get used to a school with walls again."

"Hey, today is not the day to stress," I said, even though I was already feeling a knot in my stomach about what I had to tell him. Diego admitting he needed to readjust to Luther felt like the first true glimpse of old Diego I'd seen this summer. "It's a **LAZY** river, after all."

"True," Diego said. "I so need this!"

"Me too," I said. We linked arms and took our tubes to the entry of the lazy river, which was sort of a slow-moving chute that spit you out onto the water.

"Hey, Katy's invited to the birthday party, right? And Johnny?" Diego asked as our inner tubes lulled out onto the twisty river.

"Of course!"

We started going through the list, which had gotten way bigger than what it would have been just one summer ago, and then we went over the activities. It was the most Diego had talked about having a plan with me in **FOR-EVER**. He was really into the details of the endless Wiffle ball game I'd thought up. And then we talked about how we needed to send the evite as soon as possible. He didn't once say, "Let's play it by ear."

We floated some more, our inner tubes side by side, and it was like a time machine into all our summers before: the smell of too much chlorine and the hot sun and the nice cool water on my back sort of put a spell on me. It was a lot like the Fourth of July had been, with Johnny and Diego on the blanket: like, this was **FOR SURE** an MVP Summer moment but it was so good that I didn't want to say it and snap the spell.

So Diego snapped it. "It kind of stinks that school will start soon. But I'm excited to see what no-asbestos Luther looks like. And smells like. I wonder if they painted."

"It's probably still baby-poo yellow."

"Yeah, but it's home." Oh no. I had to tell him about Piper Bell, spell or not.

"So, I got a letter yesterday," I said. "From Piper Bell."

Diego lifted his head from its reclined position. "Oh really? What about?"

"They . . . well, the school. Um. I got a scholarship. To go there. In the fall." There should have probably been a rule about not delivering life-changing news while in the water because my stomach felt queasy.

Diego's eyes got wide and he paddled toward me in the water. Then he offered his hand for a . . . high five? He was happy? "Way to go!" he said.

I just stared at his raised high-five hand.

"Come on, high five! This is awesome, Gabby!" he said. "You're going to go to Piper Bell! That's amazing.

HIGH FIVE ?!?

Wait till I tell Mom!"

Huh?

He hadn't even flinched.

He didn't even care. No, he was excited! He'd high-fived us being **SEPARATED** for eighth grade. He had his birds and his new bird friends and Katy liked him and Johnny liked him and he probably didn't even care. He probably would have been fine going back to Costa Rica a million miles away, to leave me behind **FOREVER**.

He'd probably high-five me and tell me to send a post-card.

And, for maybe the first time in my entire life, I was angry at him. I wanted to say, "This is okay with you? You don't care about our friendship?"

I'd never been mad at him before. I wished there was a way to make him feel how awful his high five had made me feel.

"Hey, I rescheduled the bird outing for the day after tomorrow, if you want to come," Diego said. **JUST CHANGING THE SUBJECT**, like we weren't going to different schools after twelve-plus years of friendship.

I wished birds had never been invented. In my most serious voice, I said, "I don't want to see another bird in my entire life. But you have fun."

It was mean. It was awful. Diego's face went from smiling to a confused frown. But I didn't apologize. If Diego didn't care enough about our friendship to be a little sad, then what was the point anyway?

My bird comment, of course, looked like it had hurt. Only because I'd insulted birds, though. I unlazily guided my inner tube to the nearest exit chute. Then I watched Diego drift away. It seemed appropriate. Or what he wanted, anyway. To drift away.

Of course, now I'm just sitting here under an umbrella with Louie waiting for Peter and Jared and Diego to return. I said I had a stomachache. It's not a lie, even if it's not from anything I ate. And, oh yeah, I can't wait to get home and cry.

The **MVP SUMMER** is over.

MVP Summer Points: 10, only because I didn't cry in front of Diego, and subtract 100 because of everything else

MVP Summer Tally: 730, minus one best friend

IT'S OUR PARTY

MVP Summer Goal: Erase the awful lazy-river moment from Diego's memory

MVP Summer Action: Bring my A game to party planning

Post-Day Analysis:

July 18

It had been four days since the awful Lazy River moment. Four rotten days because I hadn't said anything about my nasty bird comment but Diego hadn't tried to tell me what was wrong, either. But today, we were going out with our moms to party plan, and I thought if I showed up and tried to be **NICE**, we could maybe figure things out.

Party planning was supposed to be **FUN**. Not as fun as the actual party but like a preview of fun to come.

But between Diego more or less cheering that we'd go to different schools and me trying to say the meanest thing I could think of, the birthday party was feeling like a farewell party.

"Hey, how did the bird outing go?" I asked on the ride to the stores. Johnny had gone and I already knew, sort of, that Diego had created a game called Bird Bingo, which might have been fun. I hoped my interest would clear the air: I wanted to use party planning to make things feel normal again. And maybe Diego would admit that he was really sad about heading to separate schools.

"Oh yeah, it was great," he said, on the other end of the seat and looking out the window. "You wouldn't have liked it, though."

Was he mad? Sad? I couldn't tell for sure except that we weren't really talking. So there we were, riding in Diego's mom's van as she and Louie chattered away in the front seat about coupons and errands they'd be running and the rental fee for the park where we'd have our party (really boring grown-up stuff; maybe there *was* something worse than turning thirteen). In the back seat, though, this was us:

Bob and Judy were having a field day with it.

Judy: *It's quite the standoff between these longtime allies. We've been so used to them playing on the same team, I have to admit, I don't know what to make of this.*

Bob: *From the scowls on their faces, I don't think Gabby and Diego do, either.*

Judy: *The view from here looks like we're all in for a bumpy ride!*

The ride itself wasn't bumpy but it did seem like Diego and I were playing a game of who could look up from their phone the least. I was totally breaking my phone rules but if he was going to do it, so was I.

TAPTAPTAP. He pressed send on a message. To who?

So I **TAPTAPTAPPED** my own message, to Katy. "What's up?" And, I sent Johnny a message that said "Have an awesome day!" with a paintbrush because he'd mentioned helping his sister with the art camp she was a counselor for.

No one answered right away. It was early. But Diego was typing furiously. Maybe a message to Johnny or Katy. Maybe they knew I had been mean about birding and decided to choose Diego over me. But Diego had been kind of mean, too! He's basically high-fived me out of his life. Stupid phones! They made it so easy to be mad in a way that didn't seem mad, so that you could be mad at someone your whole life and never figure it out because you had things to do on your phone.

Then we pulled into a parking spot at the party store and Diego's mom said, "Phones away! It's shopping time."

Louie clapped her hands, excited. She had a small clipboard of to-do lists. Louie loves clipboards almost as much as she loves to-do lists. I think she does yoga just to clear her mind so she can write new to-do lists.

Our moms were out of the car and tapping their feet waiting for us. Diego and I each kind of oozed out of the car with less enthusiasm than things that actually ooze.

NON-ENTHUSIASTIC OOZING CREATURES

- Snails (slow-moving due to bad attitudes?)

- Worms (I think they really like their lives in the

dirt but I get the strong sense they should want more for themselves)

- Jellyfish (beautiful and mesmerizing but I read they don't really have brains so how excited are they about life, really?)

- (Side note: How do I know so much about oozing creatures? Much more than I do about birds.)

So there Diego and I were, with about as much pep to do our big birthday party prep session as two snails with really bad attitudes, and we trudge-oozed behind our moms into the store.

I had no idea how Louie and Mrs. Parker didn't notice but I think they were so wrapped up in their mission that we could have not even been there.

HAVE TWO PEOPLE ⊐EVER⊏ BEEN THIS ANGRY AT A PARTY STORE ?!?

"Okay," Mrs. Parker said. "I think if we're going to play endless Wiffle ball, we'd better buy extra bats because those things always bend. And then if we have extras, we can give them out as favors."

"Great idea," Louie said, and we marched toward the summer gear aisle. Endless Wiffle ball had been my idea, since we were having the party at the park ballfield between our cul-de-sacs. The game would be able to go on the whole time, even as people did other things, and we wouldn't keep score or anything, just play in one big glorious circle until sundown.

"I just don't know if that many people want to play Wiffle ball," Diego said. "What's the point?"

UGH. He knew what the point was! Four days ago, he was all for the game idea. "Well, Water Balloon Warfare is only going to last about five minutes," I said. "No matter how many balloons you have, they're all gone in no time. So people will need something to do."

The massive water balloon fight had been Diego's idea, and I knew he had more of a strategy in mind than just putting out a bucket of balloons and letting people fire away. (They were going to be hidden in special areas that you could find by clues, so the whole thing took on a secret-mission kind of feel. I knew it would be fun, but

I wanted to say something rotten about his idea since he'd done it about mine.)

"Okay, well, if those ideas don't work anymore," Louie said, standing in front of a Frisbee display like she was giving a speech at work, "what do you suggest?"

She had on her Common Sense Louie face, a face that meant she wasn't about to give us the good idea because we were acting like people who should have had their own good idea. (Louie was a big believer in not allowing me or Peter to complain about things unless we could find a better way.)

DON'T UPSET ← THE LADY WITH THE CLIPBOARD ↓

COMMON SENSE

"Those ideas are fine," I said.

"Yeah, they'll work," Diego said.

"Wow, are we throwing you two a birthday party or making you walk the plank?" Diego's mom asked. "Either you're not excited about this or you're already acting like teenagers."

I could have said something like, "There's no way I'm going to have a birthday party with **HIM**!" But the truth was, I didn't want to stay **MAD** at Diego. I wanted to have our party and I wanted everything to be like it was.

Didn't Diego want the same thing? Or did he have enough without me in his life?

"Okay, let's get this stuff and go order your cake, then," Louie said, looking at her binder and frowning slightly, probably because we had thrown off the timing she had had in mind.

"We're still getting a split-level with angel food and strawberry for Diego's side and chocolate with vanilla icing for Gabby's, right?" The split-level cake was something we'd come up with at a sleepover because best cake flavors weren't something we could agree on or even compromise on. Because I thought strawberry filling made the cake all gross and soggy, and Diego thought chocolate cake was boring.

Since we'd always planned on a shared birthday cake we decided we'd split it down the middle, flavor-wise.

"Maybe we should just get cupcakes," I said, knowing that Diego found cupcakes fine but mostly unexciting. "That way, everyone can just have the flavor they want."

I don't know what I wanted to happen. I guess for Diego to say, "We can't do that! It's too important. We have a **PLAN**!"

But instead, he said, "Maybe that's a good idea." Like he was **JUST FINE** with unexciting cupcakes, or a party that seemed like a funeral for our friendship.

HERE LIES
THE
FRIENDSHIP
OF
GABBY AND DIEGO
KILLED
BY A HIGH FIVE

"Well, we could do a cake that's part bird-themed and part baseball-themed," I offered. It wasn't the original plan, and I didn't know where the idea had come from, but I was fumbling for a peace-making olive branch.

"Nah," Diego said, and I couldn't even tell if he was mad or sad or just bored to be there. "Cupcakes are good. Then everyone can stick to what they like."

Oof. He'd snapped my olive branch in half.

Louie and Mrs. Parker shared a look. "If that's what you want, it's probably easier," Louie said, and I could tell she and Diego's mom were starting to wonder what was up. "Mrs. Parker and I will figure it out."

At least there was that. Someone to figure it out.

Because Diego and I didn't seem like we were going

to. But fine, if he wanted to be mad, I would be, too. We could agree on that.

MVP Summer Points: MINUS 50, at least. I'd take points away from Diego, too, if I could!

MVP Summer Tally: 680, and not looking like the season's going to be a winner

PREDATOR COMPETITOR: A REPLAY

Post-Day Analysis:
July 19

Today, I was hungry for a win.

I know, I know, I'm supposed to have a more Zen attitude and play hard but know what really matters, etc., and so on and blah blah blah.

But a win would put our team closer to a trophy and I felt like a trophy might distract me from all the questions I had. Plus, trophies meant you could be sure of one question: had you played well enough to win a trophy? Yes.

Diego wouldn't be covering my game. Johnny couldn't make it. There was a junior staff picnic for the *Gazette* that Johnny had invited me to (I was sad not to be going with him but kind of glad I didn't have to see Diego). "I'm sorry

I'll miss your game," he'd texted. "But I'll tell Katy and Diego you said hi." I wanted to tell him to only say hi to Katy but then I'd have to get into the whole thing. I didn't have time for that.

So, back to the game. I was like a shark. Okay, a shark with real bones and arms and legs and the ability to survive on land.

I was probably pretty scary. But the focus was what I needed.

Because if I wasn't focused, I had to think about everything else.

Like: Why didn't my best friend care we'd be going to separate schools? Why was everyone okay with always playing everything by ear and never planning things? Also, shouldn't there be some kind of warning if your best friend goes away for six months and comes back and is totally different? The whole point of having our best summer before we turned thirteen had been to avoid all this stuff. But Diego had clearly forgotten that. Or didn't care. I don't know which.

I didn't know. I still don't know.

What I do know is that sometimes, it's okay to be angry. At least on the field.

I didn't even care I was playing catcher. I didn't trudge

out to the position or complain or grumble. I just laser-beamed my way to my spot and got in my crouch. Ready to win.

I could have been pitching, the way I felt like I was directing the game. Alfonso was doing great on the mound. But unlike the day when the game had been his, today it was because he was too scared to shake off my signals. I think.

Our opponent was good. The Birchholt Bears. They had great hitters, in particular. Even Alfonso couldn't keep them from getting on base. But I was playing like that Rhinos catcher I'd observed at regionals. Except angrier.

When the Bears' best hitter—he was an eighth grader known for huge home runs—stepped up to the plate, I made a point to throw the ball back to Alfonso quickly and shot him a call for a curve. He threw a decent one but it didn't drop enough and the batter still managed a hit, but only a single.

Then, when I was up to bat in the third, I caught a glimpse of their catcher. It was the girl from the Rhinos. The positive, happy catcher. "Hey," I said to her even though I usually don't talk to opponents. It just came out. Because today, she didn't look like the positive beam of light she'd been back in May.

"You're one of the pitchers from Piper Bell . . ." she said to me. "The really happy one."

"Uh-huh," I said, realizing she'd **THOUGHT** I was the happy one back then. Does everyone think everyone is happier than them, even when they're happy?

Maybe closing in on teenagerdom put everyone in a bad mood. Somehow, I felt better knowing this. "You're up," she said. And I was So. UP.

I clocked a hit off a fastball to far left field. I plowed past the first baseman and made it to second. My killer instinct must have been contagious because Devon walloped a hit and batted me in. From there, the whole game went like that. Nothing got past me. I ended the ninth by diving to catch a bad throw Casey made from second base and stretching my right leg so I tagged up home just before the Bears' batter crossed the plate.

By the end of it all, I was sore and dirty and my uniform was plastered to my body with sweat. It was my best game of the season, from a playing standpoint. Coach Hollylighter and Coach Daniels told me how great I'd done, but Coach Hollylighter paused when she saw my face. "You okay?" I just nodded. What would I tell her anyway?

I'd played like a hungry shark, and I was that much

closer to a trophy. But I remembered that sharks swim alone. And for a split second, I thought being a bird would be better. They flock together.

Points suspended until cloudy angry mood subsides.

UP IN THE AIR

MVP Summer Goal: Be in a bad mood without ruining the MVP Summer (if I haven't already)

MVP Summer Strategy: Pretend I'm not in a bad mood, caused by a life crisis, brought on by the end of an important friendship?

Post-Day Analysis:
July 21

"Just remember, you can't control everything," my dad is saying. "Marcus Aurelius said, 'Remember you have power over your mind—not outside events. Realize this, and you will find strength.'"

My dad isn't giving me advice. He's stationed next to me on the couch on his laptop and murmuring Marcus

Aurelius quotes to himself because he's in what he calls The Home Stretch of his work project. But jotting it down, I wonder if the quote could also apply to me. Had Marcus been having a Summer Gone Wrong? Had Marcus Aurelius, who was dead, ever felt like he was losing his best friend? Had Marcus Aurelius ever been told—even if he was good at saying smart things people's dads would one day repeat—that he had to go write funny limericks or something? (Which was basically the same thing as being a pitcher forced to play catcher.)

I'm still going to the Summer Daze Carnival. Johnny had invited me and I figure maybe, even if he never holds my hand again and even if he doesn't like me like me, I like him like him enough for both of us. And, okay, maybe a carnival will be the romantic scenario to make him hold my hand again. Because that had been a summer highlight (clearly: I can't stop mentioning it!) and I'm not even saying that because the rest of the summer has been a little meh.

As I wait to leave to meet him, I'm staring at the TV but only now do I realize my dad is watching . . . basketball. Basketball? In July?

"What are you watching?" I ask him. He doesn't look up from his work.

"Classic basketball! Nineteen-nineties Chicago Bulls. I think this is from the 1997 finals."

Watching Michael Jordan play is like my dad's version of comfort food. Well, comfort food is also his version of comfort food, which explains the football-sized burrito on the table in front of him. Koufax looks jealous.

The sound of my dad's keyboard clacking sort of lulls me away from some of my worries about Diego. On the screen, Scottie Pippen is taking the ball toward the hoop and then passes to Michael Jordan, who goes up for a graceful layup.

Someone on the screen called a basketball historian comes on and says, "For many years of the Bulls Dynasty, Jordan and Pippen were the dynamic duo, with Jordan as the obvious leader and Pippen his own force to be reckoned with, but often not the teammate calling the shots."

Hmm. It sounds kind of familiar.

"When Jordan retired, Pippen admitted that, while he'd miss his teammate, he was looking forward to the chance to be top guy."

Hmm again. Maybe Diego and I are like Michael Jordan and Scottie Pippen. I guess for years I **HAD** called the shots. And I'd been waiting for him to ask me what the plan was this summer. I'd done new things and made new friends while Diego was gone and I'd expected him to come back and be exactly the same.

And instead, he'd become Top Guy. That had to be it.

Am I jealous? Is that what's going on? (*Writing pause while I think on this*) No. I'm not.

I can be okay with Top Guy Diego. Right? I mean, it had been pretty okay that game when Alfonso took the win, and I was just his backup guy. I don't have to be Top Guy!

But what if Diego won't give me a chance to show him that?

The TV just froze up. "Can you hit the reset button on the box, Gabs?" my dad is saying through a mouthful of burrito. His manners go out the window when he's busy.

"Sure." (*Pause as I do my dad this favor*) And with the button push the TV went black and came back on, unstuck. Why was it so easy to make the TV unstuck, but not so easy to do it with a friendship? Too bad there's not some massive life reset button to just erase all the icky stuff.

Ooh, it's time to go. I definitely don't want to reset anything before my maybe-date.

(*Pause for potential hand-holding and definite funnel cake*)

LIFE RESET BUTTON

LIFE RESET

I was a little preoccupied with making face-to-face peace with Top Guy Diego when I went to meet Johnny at Summer Daze. But, he was holding two funnel cakes and it kind of helped me stop racking my brain. The boy I liked holding one of my favorite foods seemed like some kind of sign from the Romantic Powers That Be. Also, it made me smile even if a few minutes before I didn't want to smile.

"I hope you like funnel cake," he said, handing me a plate. I decided that, even if I don't know much about dating, a date that started with fried, powdered-sugar-covered dough was a winner.

"I do," I said, remembering to answer before cramming a large hunk of dough in my mouth. Maybe that wasn't polite date behavior but it's impolite to the funnel cake not to treat it like you're extremely glad to have it. "Thank you." (I waited until my mouth wasn't full to say that.)

"Diego told me about your whole plan to come here and eat funnel cakes until you burst, so I kind of knew," he said, then reached to brush some powdered sugar off my shoulder. Which gave me the spinny cotton-candy feeling on top of the sugary funnel-cake goodness. "But I wasn't sure you'd want to get one, since you guys are on the outs."

 Diego had told him? Oh no. Also, "on the outs" sounded

so final. Was there any hope to fix something that was "on the outs"?

I must have looked sad or strange because then Johnny said, "Sorry, I guess I just feel caught in the middle." He looked down at his sneakers—a new blue pair. "I like you both."

Maybe this was meant to ease my mind but it just made me think of a new question: Did this mean he liked me liked me, or just liked me the same way he liked Diego? Maybe he like liked Diego and only liked me! How could anyone feel like they knew anything ever?

"I know," was what I said instead of asking, and then devoured another section of funnel cake, which Johnny did as well. So, he was definitely aware of funnel-cake protocol.

I pointed to the bumper cars. "Should we go on some rides?" I didn't want to talk too much about Diego because I wanted to maybe get to sit next to Johnny at some point, so that hand-holding would be easier to do. If he wanted to.

But we just went on ride after ride! Still, bumping cars, and Tilt-A-Whirling, and even hurtling in circles on the Zipper (I did not throw up) were definitely good ways to clear your head. Any less-than-positive thoughts you had seemed to fall right out of your ears. And not thinking too much with someone you thought about a lot was really nice.

Then Johnny suggested the Ferris wheel. I'm not a huge fan of Ferris wheels. They go too slow and make you look down for too long.

But I said, "Sure, how bad could it be?" while thinking it could be extremely bad. Still, it WAS an extended period of time where he could maybe hold my hand.

There was no line, and within a minute, we were going around and around and sitting shoulder to shoulder with our hands in our **LAPS**! "I think I'm supposed to say, look how small everything is from up here!" I said.

And Johnny said, "Can I tell you something?" And I nodded and my stomach got wonky—wonkier, really—and I wondered if he was going to say he didn't like me like me.

That would be awful. But then something extra-awful happened.

The Ferris wheel got stuck. This was the opposite of fun and light because: (1.) Ferris wheels weren't exactly my favorite ride in the first place; (2.) Being trapped in a swinging cage with someone who liked you but you weren't sure liked you liked you (even if you originally thought they did) was awkward and what if he was about to break up with me and then we had to **SIT HERE**?

We were at the tippy-top. Every tiny gust of wind made the cage sway back and forth in a gentle but really terrifying way. My funnel cake decided to glue itself together in a heavy ball at the bottom of my stomach. Next to me, I noticed Johnny also looked a little green.

"Are you okay?" I said.

He smiled with his lips pressed tight. "What I was about to tell you is that I'm actually kind of afraid of Ferris wheels."

"Me too!" I said. "This is my worst nightmare coming true."

He looked even more green. "So this will be the worst date ever?"

Date. That word. But this time I couldn't just let it go flying off into the breeze. I knew we probably weren't going to die, but since the chances seemed higher every time I heard the ride creak and groan, I had to ask:

"Why did you only hold my hand at the movies for a minute and then never again?"

It was like the Ferris wheel had some kind of power for making me ask something that had been bugging me all summer.

"Oh, um, I . . . well, I didn't know if you liked me. Like that," Johnny said. "I thought you would rather be getting more popcorn than holding hands."

Darn me and my nervous snacking! But also, why hadn't I just **ASKED**?? Or just asked Diego about our friendship? I

255

was so scared of hearing an answer I didn't want that I'd made myself go bananas wondering what it was.

"Of course I do," I said. "But I thought maybe you didn't like me so much, or as friends. And maybe like being friends with Diego more and you're just being nice to me?" Suddenly, I was asking all my questions.

A breeze rocked us again but this time I was more nervous about what I'd just said than the possibility of falling to our doom.

"I like Diego a lot," Johnny said. "But I also like him because you like him. And because he likes you. Simple math." He grinned a little. He sure loved math.

"Well, he doesn't anymore."

"I don't know," Johnny said. "Some things are constants. I think you and Diego will always be awesome friends, even if the variables around you might change." He blushed. "Was that really weird?"

I shook my head. "No, it was really cute. And, wait, when you said you liked Diego because I liked him and he liked me . . ."

"I meant because I like you," Johnny said. "A lot."

I looked down. And, this time—with the **ULTRA**-fuzzy **ULTRA**-flossy sensation of Johnny saying he liked me—**A LOT**—it was pretty nice: the game booths and smaller rides and parents with popcorn and kids wearing glow necklaces. The sky was kind of a pretty orange.

Like Marcus Aurelius said, my mind was made up to enjoy this. The MVP Summer wasn't something I could control or plan. Because all my favorite moments this summer hadn't been ones I'd scheduled perfectly or listed out. The MVP Summer wasn't something I could **MAKE HAPPEN**. It was something I could **JUST HAVE HAPPEN**, as long as I paid attention when it did.

There **WAS** one thing I could make happen, though. I reached out and held Johnny's hand.

"I'm glad you did that," he said.

"Me too," I replied.

A few minutes later, the Ferris wheel started to move.

I didn't mind that it took a while before I was on solid ground again.

MVP Summer Points: 100! FOR SURE!

MVP Summer Tally: 780. No way am I going to hit 1,500 but maybe part of Summer MVP-dom is knowing the best part is getting to try at all?

BIG GAME GREATNESS:
A REPLAY

Post-Day Analysis:
August 6

How was it possible that summer had the longest days but always went faster than any other time of year? Summer was coming to an end.

A funny thing had happened: It turned out, I was not such a bad catcher. Devon was not such a bad shortstop. And, whether she and I liked it or not, Casey and Alfonso were doing pretty well as pitchers. We'd somehow won four of the six we'd played, but even more, I felt like a better player.

Coach Hollylighter had had a point. And was maybe the tiniest bit smug about all of it. In one way, it was annoying how right she'd been, but in another way, I was all for enjoying whatever pleasant surprises I could get. That was sort of something I learned through the MVP Summer. I hadn't made up with Diego **YET**. I felt like we both needed time. And, on that front, I did think I needed to wait for the right moment. I would know when it came. I hoped.

"Great work, team," Coach Hollylighter said before we took the field for our last game. "I know it's hard to step outside your comfort zone, but I think you all learned something about looking at things from a different point of view."

"But we're down a couple people today," Coach Daniels went on. "So we're going to put your adaptability to the test. Devon, you're pitching so Casey can play catcher. Gabby, you're taking over at shortstop. Mario, you're back on first."

"Sweet!" Mario and Devon said at the same time.

For the splittest of seconds, I wanted to say, "Why can't I pitch **JUST TODAY**?" But that would have kind of destroyed the whole what-you've-learned thing Coach Hollylighter had said.

Maybe, like this season, I had to get used to things switching around. I was going to be thirteen tomorrow, after all. I'd told Piper Bell yesterday that I was accepting the scholarship.

So I took my place at shortstop feeling pretty good. From this vantage point, I could see each of Devon's pitches. I could see most of my teammates—except the ones in the outfield, but I could **SENSE** them.

And something weird happened. The sun seemed to be shining on me in a new way. **OLD ME**, when you read this, you might think it sounds batty (ha! Batty, at a baseball game!) but I think, sometimes you feel **CONNECTED** to everything. And, no, this is not something I stole from one of Louie's Self-Help Magic La-La books (I can't remember the titles). I think it was just a magical baseball moment.

But also an MVP Summer moment. Again. And I realized, it wasn't about what was happening outside of me, or anything I'd planned or steered in the right direction. It was about what was going on **INSIDE**.

I was like a **GOOD VIBE MACHINE**.

Like, at professional games, those people that shoot T-shirts out into the crowd from a cannon? That was me! Except instead of shooting out T-shirts, I was shooting good vibes all over the field, to all my teammates. And everyone in the stands: My parents. Johnny and his sister. Katy and the talent squad. Even Peter could have some. Ha, he probably needed them more than anyone.

I was really feeling like it was going to be a great, great game.

Then I looked around and saw Diego behind the backstop with his notebook, jotting things, and I had a flash of sadness. How had we barely talked in weeks? Still, he was HERE. That had to mean something. He squinted out over the field and I thought he might have looked right at me and smiled but it was also possible it was just a squinting-into-the-sun smile.

It would have been nice to shoot good vibes right over to Diego and be done with all the weirdness or just to go hug him and say, "You're Top Guy and that's great!" but I knew it wasn't that easy. And I also knew I had a game to play. I had to stay in the moment, until the right moment.

The first batter for the Oak Grove All-Stars came up and hit Devon's first pitch. Understandable, since Devon hadn't pitched a game this season. I watched the ball zip past her, just out of reach of her glove, and her usual glinty-eyedness changed to a panicked worry face. "I got it!" I said to her and dove to catch the ball before it dropped lower.

"Whew, thank you!" Devon said to me. I gave her the thumbs-up. She didn't need to worry. My head was fully in this game.

Devon got her head together and struck out the next batter, and the third batter hit a grounder almost right to first. The game was going our way!

By the fourth inning, we'd scored three runs to Oak Grove's one. The whole team had finally found its groove, and that baseball magic was happening for us. The team was sharing a brain. We were unstoppable.

But maybe not.

In the fifth, with a runner on first, Oak Grove's best batter hit a grounder between first and second.

Ryder lunged for it and I covered second base, expecting Ryder to throw it to me so I could tag the first-base runner out and throw to first for the double play. But Ryder must have tuned out because he threw straight to first and we only got one out on the play.

Nerves flickered inside of me. Was this what happened all the time? One second, you thought you knew exactly what someone would do, and the next, they were doing something totally different? I looked over to Diego, who was making notes and didn't look up.

In the seventh, Devon was looking tired. But so was Oak Grove. They had a player on first and their pitcher was up to bat. Devon wound up and threw the pitch. The batter bunted. Like a flash, Devon grabbed it, turned, spotted me, and threw. She could have thrown to Ryder, but he was watching the batter and not covering the base as well as he should. The throw was perfect, like there was a string between me and Devon for it to travel on. I tagged up second and easily tossed it to first. Double play!

But more importantly, maybe connections didn't change just because you made an error, like Ryder had. Maybe it was just you had ups and downs and things flipped on you sometimes. Maybe sometimes someone else had to be the center of the action, and you had to catch whatever they threw at you, because it was important. If you could do that, you were Top Guy, even if someone else was on top.

We won the game. I didn't get to see Diego before he left, and I was sad I wasn't going to get to fix everything right then and there.

But as I was packing up my gear, Coach Hollylighter said, "Gabby, I'm really proud of you this season. If we could give someone an MVP award this summer, you would have won it today."

For Coach Hollylighter to say a thing like that really meant something. It gave me the idea that everything was going to be just fine. But I still had to ask:

"So, have you heard anything about which All-Star team is getting the trophy?"

She didn't answer right away. "I'm sorry," I said. "It's about teamwork, not trophies. I know."

She grinned. "Don't tell anyone, but I **LOVE** getting trophies." Then she whispered to me, "And with this win, I think we have this one in the bag."

MVP Summer Points: 100!

MVP Summer Tally: 880, plus wisdom (trophyless . . . for now)

GARCIA AWES AND AWESOME, MAKES MVP PLAYS
BY DIEGO PARKER

Hometown hero and all-star pitcher Gabby Garcia collected two new titles in yesterday's Atlanta Area All-Stars matchup of the Peach Tree Pirates and the Oak Grove Originals: superstar shortstop and unofficial team MVP.

In a winning double play, Garcia, along with pitcher Devon DeWitt and first baseman Mario Salamida, all classmates at Piper Bell Academy last school year, fended off Oak Grove's potential game-winning offensive drive in a startling double play that makes this sportswriter think the three teammates have achieved baseball ESP. Like Georgia's state bird, the brown thrasher, Garcia in particular seemed to have endless notes at her disposal, and the songs she sang were all victorious. Thanks to her quick thinking and great communication, the Peach Tree All-Stars came away with a fantastic 7–3 victory.

After the win, Coach Regina Hollylighter said Garcia deserved an MVP award on the season: "Even if plays don't go well, she always tries to do the right thing, and she often seems to know that a mistake is not the end of the world. Gabby helps everyone look good, and she always tries to do better."

THE MEET IN THE MIDDLE:
A REPLAY OF AN EPIPHANY!

Pre-Birthday Party:
August 7

Diego couldn't have given me a better present than the story in the day's paper. Not just because he'd written about me so nicely but because I could tell that he actually cared. He'd compared me to a bird, after all. Maybe I hadn't lost him. Maybe if I'd done a better job knowing about his life while he'd been in Costa Rica, I wouldn't have been so caught off guard by his new Top Guy changes. Separate schools didn't have to be a friendship killer. There had to be a way to show him I'd make a better effort to keep up with him as Piper Bell and Luther students than I had when he was in Costa Rica. So, I'd spent last night making a highlight reel album of our friendship. Louie had helped me scan and arrange old photos and I wrote captions and memories.

We were supposed to be at the park ballfield at two, just before guests were going to arrive. It was the same field where we'd meet up when we were littler to play ball with all our friends from the neighborhood. We'd always met each other halfway between our houses and go together, no matter what, because half the fun of playing ball was getting to hang out together.

I wanted that feeling back.

I paced around the kitchen, where my dad was making all kinds of mini food for the party (even in the middle of our disagreeable day, Diego and I had both made the same grunting noise to agree on that: mini foods were perfection). There were tiny cheeseburgers, pigs-in-blankets, mini tacos—basically, it looked like a whole town of great small chefs had exploded in our kitchen.

My dad was even making mini arepas, which are delicious little cornmeal pouches filled with cheese or shredded beef. They're from a recipe handed down through his family and they're sort of complicated but he was loving the challenge (mostly because he'd turned in his project and had tons of **ENERGY**).

But I wasn't even there to steal food; just to pace, and also drive my dad nuts. "Are you nervous?" "Hungry?" "Did you accidentally drink coffee?" He followed me around with his wooden spoon and we became a father-daughter pacing duo.

"You're both scaring me," Peter said from his spot at the counter, where he was playing a game on the iPad.

"It's not every day I agree with Peter's rating of you, Gabby," Louie said as she reviewed her party itinerary one last time. "But yes, you're both scaring me."

My dad and I stopped pacing. And stopping seemed to send a thought

zooming right smack into the middle of my head, like a baseball headed right for the fences that gets stopped by the
scoreboard. Every light in my brain went on.

I kept waiting for Diego to ask, "What's the plan?"
instead of bringing the plan to him first. I kept waiting
to be Top Guy, and making Diego be my Scottie Pippen.

I needed to meet him in the middle. Or better, I needed
to bring the MVP Summer to **HIM**. Not the Template of
Deeds but the **FEELING**. But okay, also the Template of
Deeds, to which I added two things: a trip to the Atlanta
Zoo Bird Enclosure, and one morning of Best Friend
Bird-Watching.

(Later, still before party)

So I spend a lot of time wishing for ESP. Because really,
besides a bionic pitching arm, what could be better than
reading people's minds, or transmitting your thoughts to
other people (when you need to, not when you have the
yips, or when Bob and Judy are being extremely critical)?

Well, today, I had ESP.

Except it was with a bird.

The **WESTERN KINGBIRD**!!!

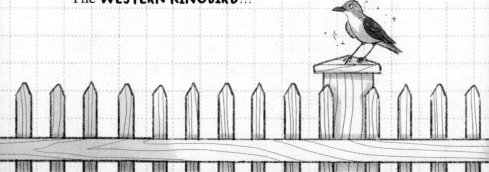

The bird Diego had been wanting to see all summer, the bird he said he had almost no chance of seeing, was just sitting there, on the fence of a house I'd never paid much attention to in my whole time of going back and forth between my and Diego's houses. I looked right at it. It bobbed its little bird head at me like it was saying, "Yes, it's me." It didn't look as mean in person.

How could I tell Diego? If I took out my phone to take a photo, the sudden movement might send the bird flying away.

It was kind of pretty, and I don't know, I guess it seemed like it knew things, or something. I wasn't going to be the bird whisperer or anything, but this bird being here, at this moment—I couldn't help it, I thought it meant something.

SMACK!

Someone ran right into me. And the first thing I did was check to make sure the bird was still there. It was. That had to qualify as extremely weird bird behavior. I sent it a silent message to stay where it was and looked to the side at the person who'd run into me . . .

. . . who was Diego.

"I didn't see you until it was too late," he said. Without saying anything, I pointed to the fence and the bird, worried for a second that maybe it wasn't the western kingbird and this wasn't the big deal I thought it was.

"Oh my gosh," he said. And the smile on his face told me that it was definitely the kingbird.

The bird tweeted a song, a sweet little thing that I swear sounded like "Happy Birthday," and then took to the sky.

"You were birding!" Diego said, pointing at me. "You do care!"

Huh?

"Huh?" I said.

"I just thought this whole time, you were changing your mind about being my friend because of the birds, or maybe because of all your new friends and stuff," he said. "But then you were **BIRDING** just now."

Was that how Diego saw things? I saw them totally different.

"I wasn't birding! The kingbird just showed up! Like a sign! But I did think that maybe I should have shown more of an interest in birds when you did." I waited for him to tell me this was absolutely true, but he shook his head.

"You don't have to. Like, you like baseball more than I do and I love Hornussen, which you don't get. The birds are just my new Hornussen."

Oh. He had a point.

"It just seemed like you changed so much and the birds

were one more thing I didn't understand," I said. "And I kept thinking we were going to have the best summer ever like we talked about when we were ten, but it seemed like you were this new person who didn't care about the plan."

"Sure I did!" Diego said. "But *you* had all this new stuff and I thought if I came back and wanted things to be like they were when we were ten, you'd think I was lame."

I showed him the Template of Deeds. "No. I had it all planned out. I was going to call it the MVP Summer."

He read down the list. "This sounds pretty awesome."

"I know!" I said. "But also, I mean, I guess I do want to plan things and every time I tried you were always busy . . ."

"But if you'd told me about this, I would have known how important it was to you."

"I wanted it to be important to you, too! And it seemed like all your new stuff was more important and then you didn't even care about me going to **PIPER BELL**!"

"I was happy for you about Piper Bell!" Diego said. "If you chose Luther just for me, I'd end up feeling bad that you missed a chance at Piper Bell. So it's easier just to be excited for you."

"Well, I should have been nicer when you became Top

Guy, but when you suddenly had so many new friends and things to do, I thought you'd forget about me."

"WHATTTT?" Diego said it just like that but it took even more letters. "No way. Never. Not a chance."

"But you don't like baseball anymore. Or want to be a sportswriter. And maybe don't want to be my best friend."

"I still like baseball **AND** I *am* sportswriting! Part of why I found new interests in Costa Rica was to keep busy while I was missing my best friend. And I ended up really liking them."

"But it wasn't very nice of me to not pay attention."

"You were fine. You had a new school to go to and everything. That's kind of harder in a lot of ways than living in a remote jungle, which is very relaxing really." Diego grinned. "And I think you're getting the MVP Summer thing a little wrong."

"Because I plan too much and get disappointed when it doesn't work out?"

"Not exactly. More because you're keeping score for a game that no one knows about but that we'd all want to play if we did."

Hmm. Of course Diego would get it, and get it better than I ever had.

"Do you mean that . . . about Luther? We'll be okay?"

"Yeah. It's just a chapter in our ESPN documentary," he said.

"You're going to be an ornithologist, though," I said. "We won't have a documentary now."

"You don't know everything," he said. "But I do know that you're my friend forever."

We hugged then. "Happy birthday," we said, and plopped down in the grass.

"I made you something," I said, giving Diego the high-light reel.

He flipped it open and was immediately impressed.

"You did all this?"

"Of course I did," I said. He started turning the pages and reading the history of our friend-ship.

Then we heard the Freezemo-bile song. "Is that what I think it is?" Diego said.

"It is!" I pointed as the Freeze-mobile turned the corner and I jumped up, waving my hands. It pulled over right in front of us, so I fished some money out of my pocket and showed Diego the spot on the list that said to try five new ice cream bars. "Maybe just two each? Since we'll be eating cake later?"

"Okay," Diego said, choosing something with a jaw-breaker in the middle (don't recommend) and a triple-chocolate ice cream taco (do recommend). I had a sherbet snowball (**NO**) and a strawberry-lemon slush pop (**YES!**).

We sat there on the curb, trying to eat our ice cream before it melted down our arms, which is very hard to do when you have an ice cream bar in each hand.

It was one of those unplanned moments that was ultimate MVP Summer material.

Diego kicked my shoe with his. "You know, I should have known you'd see the kingbird."

"Why's that?"

"'Cause when I was doing all this stuff in Costa Rica and wondering if it was weird to be so into birds and stuff, I thought, what would Gabby do?"

"And what I would do is what?"

"Just be the best birder ever," he said. "Kind of like you do everything."

It was kind of cloudy out, but I was warmer than I'd felt all summer.

MVP Summer Tally: It feels like I got 1,500 points all at once, but then I realized I don't know if it's possible to give the best MVP Summer moments any points at all. So my quest is one I'll never be finished with. I'm in for the long game! And I wouldn't have it any other way!

MY FIRST REPLAY AS AN OFFICIAL THIRTEEN-YEAR-OLD

Post-Party Analysis:
August 8

Here's something I've learned, even as I record lots of things for posterity. The best best **BEST** things are ones you won't forget, even if you don't take a million pictures or write them down perfectly. The best moments . . . are like poems. (I can hardly believe I didn't say "like baseball.") A little fuzzy, but mostly a feeling.

SOME HIGHLIGHTS FROM THE PARTY

- Johnny hit more Wiffle ball home runs than anyone I've ever known.

- Katy wrote us an original birthday song! A Katy Harris original!

- Mario and Diego bonded over their moms still treating them like they are babies (right after both their moms offered to cut their mini burgers in smaller bites).

- Molly Oliver turned out to have an additional talent: she is a natural leader of water balloon warfare.

- Devon DeWitt is very good with small children, and even does a baby-talk voice. Who knew??

Our party was a poem. We stayed at the park until way past dark. **EVERYONE** came. Family, friends. The talent squad. The all-star team. Our Luther friends. Even a Luther lunch lady who lives in our cul-de-sac. **EVERYONE**. (Well, except for the kids unlucky enough to be on vacation at Disney World or something.)

The whole thing made me feel not only like I was **A LIFE MVP** but like **EVERYONE I KNOW IS A LIFE MVP**. (Even Peter, who I caught having fun at least once.) I don't know if it gets any better than that!

THE LONG GAME

Not every day
Is a banner day
A prize day
Or even a great day
Not every game is a winner
But if you always show up
And you mostly try to smile
Things start to add up, after a while
The long game can take time
And it's never really done
But if you try to play each day
Each day is one you've kind of won

THE LAST HURRAH

MVP Summer Goal: Make! The! Most! Of! Every! Moment!

MVP Summer Action: Probably eat funnel cake!

Post-Day Analysis:

August 11

So here's another piece of wisdom I learned in my MVP Summer That Almost Wasn't. Carnivals, like Peach Tree Summer Daze, are kind of all the same. And if you go one or two towns over from your own town on any given summer weekend, you can find a carnival.

Today, Diego and I made up for missing our planned-for Summer Daze day by finding one of these carnivals.

And inviting Johnny and Katy. For a **HANGOUT**. With hand-holding.

Diego and I had ridden the Zipper at least six times in a row. It was not pretty. But it **WAS** awesome. And not entirely a bad thing because at least we hadn't feasted on funnel cakes *before* we rode. (After three rides, Johnny and Katy had offered to go get those for us.) I was still kind of dizzy when we headed to the milk bottle toss, so we opted to send Diego to the weight-guessing booth first.

The woman in charge of guessing took one look at him and said, "Look at this string bean." (Yes, Diego was still a string bean even after consuming several funnel cakes. And they must have helped, because the guesser said, "I'm going to say 85.")

She had to come within two pounds. Diego looked nervous as he stepped on the scale.

And when Diego stepped on her scale, he was 92!

He chose a huge polar bear. Then, as Katy and Johnny went to check out a water-shooting game, Diego and I walked over (well, Diego sort of skipped, he was so happy) to the milk bottle toss.

"Is it going to be weird, not going to school together next year?" I asked him as I gave the carnival worker my three dollars in exchange for five balls. (I'd probably only

JOHNNY MADDEN

FOR PRESIDENT???

need two of them to win.)

"Come on, Gabby! We've been over this. Nothing will be weird." Diego gave me a good-luck thumbs-up and I wound up for my first throw.

I knocked down three bottles. The worker set them back up. It was too bad the prizes were just stuffed animals and not another trophy to go with the All-Star trophy I'd just gotten at a ceremony that morning.

I saw Katy and Johnny coming back our way, and they must have made a stop because now their hands were full with two trays of cheese fries! We were definitely not making Good Choices today. Fun Choices, but not Good Ones. My stomach growled. I gave my next turn to a little girl who was in line, feeling like a Good Samaritan, even if the truth was I just wanted to snag a cheese fry before the cheese got all solidified. No one is perfect.

"I've been thinking," Diego said to us all as he wiped a bit of cheese from his lips. "This is the year I really want to win class president. Last year at Luther and all."

"That's crazy," I said. "I was thinking about doing the

same thing at Piper Bell!" It's true. Since I sorted myself out this summer, and thought more about all the things I've learned, I thought, why not try it?

"Wait, what did you just say?" Katy asked.

"I was thinking of running for class president. At Piper Bell." Katy looked a bit shocked.

Johnny took my hand and squinted at me, then went to straighten a tie he wasn't wearing. "Huh. So, that's weird. Because I was thinking of doing the same thing. My platform is about enhancing academics."

"Mine is about the arts," Katy said, maybe a little huffily. "We need more of them."

I didn't have a platform but suddenly I needed one. "Mine is athletics. They bring people together, and I want more people to participate, even if they're not the best players." I'd just thought of it, but it sounded good.

Diego edged into our cluster, which wasn't a happy one at the moment. "Well, we still have time before school starts. Shouldn't we just have fun?"

Thank goodness for Diego and his diplomacy skills.

"You're right," Katy said.

"Yeah, okay," Johnny agreed. "We still have tickets left. What should we ride next? Bumper cars?"

"I'm still recovering from the Zipper," I said. "You guys go ahead."

"Yeah, I don't feel so great," Diego agreed, clutching his stomach. As Katy and Johnny headed for the ride, Diego turned to me.

"Birds of a feather flock together," he said, and gave me a nervous look. "Maybe we just look at it as something we all have in common?"

He knew what I was thinking, I think.

Why was it that just when I thought I was winning at the game of life, it throws me into extra innings???

ACKNOWLEDGMENTS

If you put me on a trading card and let me pick one stat to maintain a perfect record in for the rest of my life, it would be saying thank you. Because, every day, I realize more and more that the best thing about this game of life I'm in is that I have so many people who I want to thank.

So many, in fact, that I know I'm going to miss someone here, in part due to necessity because I could fill a book with the people I'd like to acknowledge for the ways big and small they get me through the game.

Let's start with a couple heavy hitters: Claudia Gabel, my editor, has helped me make everything I've written better. With her insights, expertise, and creativity, she sometimes sees Gabby more clearly than I do, and is an all-star at getting me to find what's at the heart of the story. Stephanie Guerdan keeps me on base and running for home.

To Katie Fitch and Amy Ryan, thank you for making Gabby's books look like winners. (Gabby loves that.)

To Marta Kissi, who continues to astound me by capturing the weird ideas in my head and bringing them to life; every drawing, from the smallest margin doodle to the most detailed illustration, gives me endless joy!

To Katherine Tegen and the entire team at KT Books, especially Emily Rader, Mark Rifkin, Meagan Finnerty, and Mitchell Thorpe, thank you for the endless hard work and support.

To my agent, Fonda Snyder, who has long been a great friend to me, and who possesses not only know-how, but exemplary kindness. I'm very grateful you're in my life.

To family members and friends near and far who cheered on Gabby from the get-go. There are too many of you to possibly list, but your names are all writ large on the jumbotron of my mind.

To all the librarians, teachers, and school librarians, not only for bringing Gabby to your shelves but for everything you do to champion readers every day.

To young readers who've written me about Gabby (or whose parents have): the only thing better than seeing

Gabby books on shelves is imagining them in your hands, so thank you. A huge high five to you all.

To my parents, Bill and Debra Palmer, for knowing I could write books before I even did. Mom, I wish you could have met Gabby.

To my son Clark, who keeps asking me when the next Gabby book is coming out, thank you for being the CEO (Chief Enthusiasm Officer) in this and so many things. To my son Nathan, who makes sure that I get up from my desk and stretch a bit (often by causing something to crash in the next room). To my sons together for being such excellent friends to each other; watching you love each other is one of the best things I get to do.

To my husband, Steve Stanis, who's owed so many thank-yous for everything, from giving excellent pep talks to providing game-time refreshments to reminding me that sometimes taking a time-out is okay. I'd pick you first for my team every time.

AUTHOR BIO

Born: Evergreen Park, Illinois

Resides: Burbank, California

Height: 5'5" (and an extra three-quarters of an inch that might as well be a foot for how much she likes to point it out)

Build: Well suited for jotting down ideas on small slips of paper and misplacing them, writing fiction in rapid and not-so-rapid bursts of typing, and random dancing

Sports: Running (5Ks), reading (marathons), headstands of greater than thirty seconds, baseball (swing-for-the-fences batting cage bouts only), and basketball (heavy swagger/so-so shooting)

Excels at: daydreaming, talking to strangers, asking questions, sniffing out nearby taco trucks, being easily startled

Favorite athletes: co-daredevil sons Nathan and Clark

Closest teammate: Husband, Steve Stanis

Motto: "Sure, why not?"

GREAT BOOKS BY
IVA-MARIE PALMER!

Life just keeps
throwing curveballs.

Thank goodness Gabby
has her playbook!

KT KATHERINE TEGEN BOOKS
An Imprint of HarperCollins Publishers

www.harpercollinschildrens.com